UNSPOKEN

HATTIE JUDE

Unspoken
by Hattie Jude

Cover by Jena Brignola
Editing: Christine Estevez

For information, contact:
hattiejude@gmail.com

CHAPTER ONE

When I wake up, Raf is holding my hand. He's the only one in the room and he looks half-asleep as he stares at me. His pale blue eyes widen when he sees I'm awake. He drags his hand through his thick hair and it sticks up everywhere. How he manages to still look like a model while sitting up all night in a hospital is a mystery.

"Hi," he whispers. "Your mom is going to be upset that she's not here for this. She's been here the whole time, but she left to get something more comfortable for you to wear when you woke up."

I don't say anything, staring at the deep lines in his forehead, the red in his eyes, and the way his shoulders are sinking.

"How are you feeling?"

"Like I almost drowned." I sound like a croaking frog.

His smile is sad and it's almost soft in this moment, tender. I blink, thinking when my vision clears, I'll see the hard lines in his face again, his solid shoulders unbendable. But he looks younger and scared.

"I thought I lost you," he whispers.

A flash of how peaceful it felt when I was completely submerged in the water floats across my vision. When it clears, he's staring at me like I mean something to him.

I know better.

"Shouldn't matter since you hate me so much," I whisper back.

He rolls his eyes and his grip on my hand tightens.

"Why did you give up out there? You stopped fighting."

"What is there to fight for?" My voice breaks and I go back to whispering. "I'm not very good at living like this."

He leans down until his forehead is on our joined hands and he takes a long, deep breath. "You have everything to fight for. Please, don't ever...*ever* do that again."

"My life has never been my own." The tears fall down my cheeks now and I take a shuddering breath. "I'm tired. I wish you hadn't saved me."

He lifts his head and the agonized look on his face makes my heart drop. It turns hard as he stares at me and I take my hand from his. He sits up and then stands, any warmth I felt from him falling off in sheets of ice.

"Next time I *won't* save you," he says.

He walks out of the room and I wish I could say it makes me feel better, but it's as if my insides are being scraped out. I stare at the dark room and feel more alone than I've ever felt.

My mom and Ashton are there the next time I wake up. No one mentions Raf. They both dote over me and I feel like I'm existing in slow motion, every movement ten beats behind what they expect of me. I'm fine, I don't even know why I'm still in the hospital, other than I wanted to die.

But no one is acknowledging that, which is possibly a good thing as far as how soon I get out of the hospital. I think I have Raf to thank for that. His tall tale about me getting too tired getting "exercise" in the water worked.

When Ashton drives my mom and me home, I expect him to pull into Raf's driveway and am so relieved when he doesn't. My mom is dating Raf's dad, Stefen—the worst surprise ever—and insisted we stayed with him when we were both harmed at our house. I'd rather live in fear than stay another night in Raf's house.

My stomach drops thinking about everything that happened between us in his guest room. I can't go back there. It's hard enough to stop thinking about Raf without having to sleep in the bed where we had sex.

"Stefen installed a security system here that is as state of the art as the one at his house, so we'll be safe here," my mom says, smiling at me over her shoulder.

I smile at her, thrilled that we're going home. The thought of going back to Raf's made me wish I could rush back out to the water.

The way Ashton and Mom handle me, it seems they know I'm barely hanging on a thread of sanity. One wrong move might send me over the edge. It's both empowering and comical...and *embarrassing*. I didn't mean to create this much drama. I just wanted to forget the disaster that is my life.

I haven't talked to Ashton or my mom about the porno circulating that stars me, but I know they know and *they know that I know they know*...so there's a whole lot of AWKWARD. Not to mention that I ended up in the water with the intent of never walking out again...but no one is talking about that either.

Luke, my ex—I don't really think I can call him a

boyfriend since we never once went on a date—got sent to prison for having sex with me, a minor. The fact that he was a porn star was problematic for me only because I didn't want my porn star mother or porn director dad to find out I was sleeping with one of their coworkers. Our entire relationship consisted of me sneaking out to his house and handing my innocence to him on a silver platter. I didn't know he was recording us, and I never once thought about the fact that us having sex was illegal. It was all too exciting. Too thrilling to have a secret of my own.

And for a girl who had been ignored by wealthy, busy parents her entire life, the attention he fed me was a new kind of high. I quickly became addicted. Not just to him, but the alcohol he plied me with every time we were together.

How an old sex video of us is circulating now, after he's done his time and has resorted to leaving red lilies on my doorstep—at least, I think it's him—is a new level of low for how far my life has fallen.

My mom and I left Vegas to make a new start in Long Island, and even my dad, who promised he'd do right by us, *for once*, has left threatening notes—at least I think it's him.

But what do I know about *anything*?

Trouble has followed me here. Most of it has been because of Raf, the guy I hate more than anything, but also can't seem to keep my hands off of. And there's his sometimes side-piece, Heidi, who despises me. I've been the victim of more pranks at school than I can count, and Luke and my father were nowhere near me when that happened. I can't blame them for all the drama at Longlake Prep.

It's no wonder I wanted to get in that water and never step on land again.

My mom and Ashton get me settled in my room and are

treating me with such kid gloves that I have the thought that even Raf would be better than this. At least he talks to me the same as before.

But he doesn't show up and I don't ask for him, and after I sleep a lot and then sleep some more, I realize he might not be coming back.

Ever.

And I need to be okay with that.

Luci brings my schoolwork over and we work on homework together as I steadily recover. I've missed four days of school and have stayed off of social media, scared to know what's being said about me. And how Raf has moved on without me.

I haven't seen him since that day in the hospital.

I hear my mom talking to Stefen occasionally, but the Barrons stay away. I know it should make me feel better, but nothing does. My head is a vacuous void.

Over the weekend, my mom and I watch movies and Ashton and Luci both visit. They keep it light and conflict-free.

Until Sunday night.

It's just my mom and me and I can tell she wants to talk about something important when she sets the takeout on the table and just stands there looking in my general direction.

I pile my plate with Chinese food and wait for the bomb to drop.

"I've told the school you'll be back tomorrow. It's time you get back. If you hope to graduate—"

"I'm not going back."

"Yes. You have to. If you're serious about Columbia."

"I don't know if I'm going there anymore."

"What? You don't mean that, Jocelyn."

I cringe when she says my first name. I've gone by my middle name Gabriela or Gabi since I moved here, new beginning and all that, but Mom can't seem to adjust. It was her idea even, but I guess I will always be Jocelyn to her. She sits next to me on the couch and I keep eating. Anything to avoid looking at her.

"We've filed a lawsuit against the site that posted that video. It's been taken down," she says.

"You know it will never be gone. Once those things go up, they're out there. Forever."

"But it won't be easy to access anymore. I've hired a lawyer who will track it down every time. I'm not giving up and you shouldn't either. You didn't ask for this. I'm so sorry it happened—I will always feel responsible for it."

"None of this is your fault."

She sighs and leans her head against the couch cushions, turning to face me. "Should you call your sponsor? Is there someone else you can talk to? I don't know what to do to help."

"Don't make me go back to school." I shrug. School might be the tipping point for me drinking.

"Anything except that."

"Then don't bother acting like you want to help me."

She stands up and walks into the other room, her shoulders set in a rigid line.

The next morning Ashton and Luci show up at seven and force me to get out of bed. My head hurts and I'm struggling to wake up since I got little sleep, but they're trying so hard,

I stop fighting and give in. Maybe I can skip later in the day if it gets too hard. I don't bother with makeup and leave my hair down, wishing it covered my entire face. Anything to hide.

We ride together and they chat the whole way. When Raf's name is mentioned, I perk up, listening for the first time.

"Henry and Raf have been hanging out with Toby Matthison," Ashton says. "Did you notice anything different about Toby?"

"I didn't know him well," Luci says. "What's different?"

"I don't know. He always seemed so out of it before...I thought he'd seem that way now, but he's not. Maybe his time in the hospital got him clean." Ashton pulls into the school parking lot.

When I don't see Raf's car, I sag against the seat. I'm not ready to see him. I think about Toby and wish I'd talked to my sponsor, Laura, again, asked her what's going on there... why he'd be at my school. There were too many coincidences for him not to be her brother. He's twenty-three, obviously too old for high school, and was in a coma for Christ's sake. But things have been weird with her. She's not been checking on me and I've needed her more than ever. I thought I was past feeling like I wanted to drink, but if ever there was a time I've felt like I needed one, it's today, coming back to Longlake.

When the car stops, Ashton and Luci turn around and look at me. I opted for the backseat so I could be out of their line of sight, but it's not working now.

"Ready?" Luci smiles.

"As much as I'll ever be, I guess."

I hate my mother with a passion right now.

When I get to my locker, I open it tentatively while

Ashton and Luci stand nearby, my guard dogs. All kinds of things have been known to fall out of my locker in the past, so I'm surprised I even still use the thing.

A red lily falls out and I jump back like I've been burned. Ashton picks it up and holds it out for me, his jaw clenching. He knows I hate red lilies but doesn't know why. Chalk it up to another Luke side effect.

"Pretty," Luci whispers. "Who do you think left it?"

I'm shaking when I grab the flower from Ashton's hand and toss it in the garbage.

"Gabi? Are you okay?" I hear Luci asking me, but I rush to my class and don't look back, feeling haunted.

I hear the whispers and feel the stares all day long. Everyone has either seen the video or knows about it because when I walk by, they moan Luke's name the way I did. When I sit at my desk, when I grab my lunch...I hear their moans. My moans. The day feels endless and I haven't even made it to the halfway point.

The good news is they don't seem to know about my attempt to drown. Small blessings.

I haven't seen Raf all day, but when I do, it's after a guy I've never even talked to before walks by in the lunch room, moaning, "Luuuuuuke."

I look up in time to see Raf's fist connect with the guy's jaw and he goes down. Everyone stops talking for a few seconds and not one teacher reprimands Raf for assaulting another student. He walks me to class, not saying a word or even glancing in my direction, and he's there to walk me to the next class when that one is over. Same with the next. No one else bothers me for the rest of the day.

After the last class, he walks me to my locker and when Ashton gets there, they nod, and Raf walks out.

"What was that about?" I ask.

"Just looking out for you."

"You and Raf are getting along again?" I frown at him.

"Yeah. He still doesn't like how close you and I are, but he thinks it's best if we work together on this."

Hmm. Maybe Raf has a heart. A tiny heart, but a heart nonetheless.

Then again, it probably all goes back to what his father expects of him, but still...I'm grateful. It made the day easier.

CHAPTER TWO

Chalk it up to inexperience with a side of horny, but Luke's seduction of me was swift and once he snared me, he had me right where he wanted me. We met at my parents' Christmas party, where he sat and talked with me on the stairs instead of ever going into the actual party. That in itself won huge points with me, making me think I was so interesting that he didn't need anyone else.

At sixteen, what a joke.

The fact that he was older than me was the least of the attraction, at least that's what I thought at the time. Looking back on it now, I can see that it was part of it. The forbidden. His skill at manipulation, his way of luring me in with his attention.

All a trap.

Not long after the Christmas party, I went to my favorite coffee shop and was tucked away in a corner reading about Jericho in *Darkfever*, my hands tight against my mug of chai latte. Maybe it's because I was so turned on by Jericho—or Karen Moning's words, same difference—that I felt like fate had dropped Luke into my life at the perfect moment. He probably wouldn't have had to be even half as attractive, but fuck me, he was chiseled blond perfection.

Not even my type, but my body said another story.

"What are you reading, pretty girl?"

No *hello*, just straight to the point. All I heard was that he thought I was pretty.

Stupid, stupid girl.

I shut the book and smiled up at him and he sat across from me, staring at me with promise behind his eyes.

The next time I went to the coffee shop, he was there waiting.

And the next, and the next...

With a red lily just for me.

The first time I went to his house was also the first time he kissed me, the first time we had sex. He pulled me inside, kissing me as soon as the door closed behind us. He took the lily he'd given me, now a tradition every time he saw me, and trailed it across my skin as he took my clothes off. When we reached the bed, and I was lying before him, basking in the way his eyes glistened with lust, I thought I was in love. That *we* were in love.

Yes, he was a rapidly rising-to-fame porn star, but instead of that being a turn-off, it meant so much more that someone with that much experience would want to be with someone like me.

I gave him my virginity wrapped like a gift with a shiny red bow, all in, no reservations whatsoever.

I was ready.

He was willing.

It hurt.

Bad.

He didn't kiss me like he had at the door. There was no attention paid to my body like the love stories I read about.

He was no Jericho.

"Next time it will be better," he promised.

And I believed him.

After all, if a porn star didn't know how to make a woman feel good, no one did.

I saw a camera the second time I went to his house. There were mirrors everywhere that had distracted me before. It was while we were having sex this time that I noticed Luke watching the mirrors. I lifted my head to meet his eyes in the mirror, but he was looking at himself and the way his body moved over mine like a piston firing.

I wondered for a fleeting moment if he saw me at all. Was he picturing his costars while he fucked me? All the reasons I'd felt special vanished when I saw the camera flashing.

I put my hand on his chest and he stopped pumping into me. It was a momentary relief. I was too tense.

"Are you recording this?"

"What?" He frowned. "What are you talking about?"

"The camera over there." I pointed over his shoulder and he didn't even glance to see where I was pointing.

"No. I have a camera here for rehearsing." He grinned and leaned down to kiss my shoulder. "It takes practice to look good on camera."

"You swear it?"

"Yes, I swear it takes practice to look good on camera." He laughed.

I rolled my eyes, giving his chest another slight push. He leaned down to kiss the tip of my nose and my chest did that little flutter. This playful side of him was what had been missing since I started coming over to his house. He was acting more like he had on our coffee shop dates and I let the warmth wash through me. He did feel the same.

When he began thrusting again, I was ready. I didn't come at all, but I realized he'd been right—it was better the next time.

Third time's a charm.

The camera wasn't in the same place. I relaxed.

He gave me a sweet drink when I came in the door. Fruity alcohol with my red lily. My limbs loosened and he was all gleaming eyes and smiles. He danced with me in the living room and kissed me until I saw stars.

This. *This* was what I'd dreamed of. Finally.

When he led me into the bedroom, I stripped while he watched me appreciatively, and he took his time with me. I felt worshipped. His hands and mouth explored every part of me, and I was chanting his name before he ever plunged inside of me.

It was a completely new experience and all I'd ever wanted.

We had sex twice that day. It was after the second time, when he'd fucked me for what felt like hours, relentlessly, and I'd come time and time again, that I saw the camera in a hanging plant.

This time I saw a tiny flashing green light. It was faint

and hard to see between the leaves, but I wasn't imagining it. I shoved him off of me, his cock jutting out like an angry weapon, and I pointed at the camera.

"You're recording us. Don't lie to me, Luke." I grabbed his shirt, the first clothing I saw, and tugged it over my head.

He shook his head. "I already told you—I'm not. Believe me, baby." He came toward me, still eager to finish.

He shot me puppy dog eyes, but around his nostrils, a small line of blood trickled out. I'd heard about drugs being used for the business, but I hadn't thought my boyfriend would need it to be with me.

He was my boyfriend in my head only—who knows how he thought of himself at that point? We'd never talked about it. But after a dozen chats at the coffee shop and three visits to his house, I felt qualified to make that call.

"I have to go." I whirled around, grabbing my clothes as fast as I could.

"Baby, wait, please," he yelled.

I was almost to the door when he yanked my hair back and pulled my back to his chest.

"I didn't say you could leave yet," he said in my ear.

And that's when everything went cold inside of me.

I was well and truly fucked.

CHAPTER THREE

Leaving Vegas has helped more than I thought possible. Before my mom and I moved to Long Island, I'd been living in the constant cycle of fearfully looking over my shoulder and obsessing about how I handed Luke permission to mistreat me on a silver platter. And even though it's been stressful, wondering what Luke could be up to now, the friction with Raf is what has kept my attention.

But now, I don't know. I'm a mess. Raf is maintaining a distance and the memories are wreaking havoc on my mind again. I'm humiliated that my past can still ruin me. Will I ever be able to move on from the mistakes I made? Raf and Ashton shoot looks of confusion and trepidation at me regularly and I'm too deep in the pain of reliving everything that's happened to make it any less awkward. I feel like a child who's being shuffled between parents, the custody between two hot guys who used to be best friends coming together to watch out for me. It's weird, but it helps so much that I can't let that bother me. I get through the week and start to get caught up on my schoolwork. There are no more surprises in my locker and Heidi even stays out of my way.

I see Henry hand something off to Toby and it puts Toby back on my radar. Henry gives the packet to Amber and she tucks it away. Drugs, I'm pretty sure. I keep forgetting about Toby or I keep trying to...it feels like one too many things to focus on. I need simplicity right now. But it looked suspiciously like the harder stuff and I didn't know Raf's friend Henry was into that. He's always struck me as a smart, sarcastic guy but fairly innocent.

It bothers me all day. I see Raf at lunchtime, doing his guarding routine but not looking at me, and I step closer to him.

"Is Henry okay?"

"What do you mean?" When he glances at me, even agitated, I realize how much I've missed his eyes on me.

"I think I saw him with drugs earlier."

His jaw ticks, and this time, his eyes flash with something else. Rage and fear.

"Stay out of it, Gabi. God. What's it going to take to get through to you? Just stay the fuck out of it. Got it?"

"What? Okay. Wow. Just trying to give you a heads-up about your friend. If I saw it, I'm sure I'm not the only one around here who did. And he passed something off to Amber."

He leans across the table until I feel his breath when he speaks. "Forget you saw it. I fucking mean it. I can't afford to have you—" He shakes his head and stands up, picking up his tray and glaring down at me. "I fucking mean it. *Mouth shut.*"

My heart is thudding against my shirt and I feel more afraid of Raf than I have in a long time. What is he involved in?

Ashton sits in the newly open spot, eyes wide. "What

was that all about? It looked like Raf was yelling at you, but I didn't hear what he said."

"I don't know what his problem is. Will he ever stop being confusing?"

"Seems to be his middle name." He grins.

"He's the most annoying person I've ever met."

"More annoying than Heidi?"

"Well, no...but they do belong together."

Ashton leans in closer. "I heard her bragging to some friends that she sucked him off last weekend. All ten inches, according to her." His eyebrows lift almost as high as his hairline. "He walked by as she was talking and told everyone she was too shit-faced to get anywhere near his dick last weekend or any other weekend this year." He cackles and when I don't join him in the laughter, he stops and tilts his head. "It's hilarious. Why aren't you laughing?"

"Because I don't believe he hasn't been with Heidi since school started. He told me he was going to be with her...that same weekend she's talking about."

He shrugs. "She must've been too drunk to do it because the boy wasn't lying."

"Why would he try to make me think he's with her?"

Ashton takes a huge bite and chews it slowly, chuckling under his breath as he stares at me like it's so obvious. "I mean... why have we let him think there's something between us?"

That shuts me up.

I'm tired of it all. The games. The secrets. The unknown.

I'm tired of being at Longlake. Tired of looking over my shoulder.

And I'm absolutely exhausted with trying to fight my feelings for Raf Barron.

"Have you ever thought about doing a threesome?" Ashton says under his breath and I nearly choke.

"No," I spit out.

"Because you do it for me just as much as Raf does..."

"Ashton..." I flush and stare at my plate. "Stop. We're friends."

He grins. "Okay, but if you ever change your mind." He lifts one shoulder. "It could be fun."

"*Stop.*"

He laughs again and when I look at him again, his eyes are twinkling, and I hope that was all a joke because I don't want to have another thing to add to my list of stresses. He puts his arm around me as we walk out of the lunchroom, and it feels the same as it always does, like my friend is looking out for me.

I'd like to keep it that way.

Stefen is talking with my mom in the kitchen when I get home. He's been so scarce around here since we came back home that it feels weird to hear him now. I don't want to see him, but I need a snack, so I step into the kitchen and he stops in mid-sentence.

My mom is crying and I glare at Stefen.

"What's going on?"

She blows her nose and shakes her head. "It's nothing. Your father..."

"Has he left another note?"

Her forehead crinkles. "What do you mean? What note?"

"He left one here that day I—" I stop myself from telling

the truth about that day I tried to drown. "It was about not keeping his promises."

"Oh. Well, he's certainly not keeping his promises. I don't know why I ever thought he would." She sobs into her hand and turns to Stefen, her head leaning against his chest.

I'm glad she's not spouting anything like he loves her *too much* now. She had the audacity to tell me that the reason my father abused her all those years was because he loved her too much. And we wonder why I have no idea how to have a relationship of my own.

"You know he could've kept that video of you from ever being seen," she says through her tears, "and I will never ever forgive him for letting it get out."

My mouth drops. I don't know why I haven't thought of it. "You think that was him? Not Luke?" I put a hand to my chest and then hold onto the counter for support. I thought there was a line my father wouldn't cross. "Are you sure?"

"Well, Luke is responsible for filming without your consent. Or did you know he was recording?" She looks at me sternly for a moment and my mouth drops.

"Of course I didn't know! Not until it was too late."

But I think back to how I wondered from the beginning if he was recording, how I believed his lies. I'm ashamed I didn't get out of there the first time I wondered.

"I had to ask. And the answer is *yes* about your father," she whispers. "I'm sorry, but you need to know what he's capable of. I've tried to keep the worst of it from you, even though I know you saw a lot of it in...our home."

I can't listen anymore. I turn and bail out of the kitchen and up the stairs, slamming my door shut. I hear her outside my door within seconds, but I've locked it.

"Gabi, open the door. Please, don't do anything crazy. I shouldn't have told you. Open up."

"Leave me alone. I just need..." I collapse onto my bed and crawl under the covers, piling them over my head.

I didn't want to die the day I walked into the water. Not at first. It wasn't until I experienced the quiet stillness that took over when I let the water take me that I wanted to have that feeling forever.

I need to stay far away from the water now because if I get near it, I'll never come out again.

I don't leave my room for the rest of the night and when Raf pounds on my bedroom door the next morning, along with Ashton and Luci, I surprise them all when I open the door and am ready to go. I look like shit if their response is anything to go on. Luci's mouth opens and closes and she reaches out to pat my arm. Ashton asks if I need a little more time and Raf says nothing. He takes in everything, though, from my red-rimmed, puffy eyes to my baggy sweat-shirt in place of my school blazer.

Ashton sees my blazer hanging on my chair and grabs it. "You'll need this." He winks.

Ashton and Luci try to make Raf and me smile all the way to school. They don't admit it, but I think they're enjoying the challenge, each working off of the other to one-up the stakes. Luci starts rapping and when Ashton sings an alternate show tune melody as Luci takes a deep breath, I can't help but laugh. It sounds forced and fake, but it's all that comes out.

"That's a start," Ashton whispers when he's done singing.

I smile at him and reach in the backseat to take his hand, admiring the way my pale skin looks against his dark, muscled arm. Raf turns and stares pointedly at me, as if he's betrayed or something. I don't bother trying to figure it out. When we get to school, Luci and Ashton flank me on either side and Raf walks ahead of us. We're given a wide berth as we make our way down the hall and I wonder what Raf had to do to get everyone to shut their mouths about me. They're not laughing at me now.

I know what they're capable of, but I'm grateful I don't have to hear it out loud, at least not today. I get through my classes with minimal conflict. Heidi can't seem to help herself. She's like a pesky gnat that won't go away. I ignore her jabs and she gets more agitated the more controlled I am.

In the locker room before gym, I'm nervous about being around the girls without Ashton or Raf covering for me, but Heidi's little group hovers around her locker after they've changed. I see Heidi pass something off to Jen, and Amber shakes her head no and backs up. I've never seen any of them go against Heidi, so it catches my attention more than anything, the disgust on Amber's face. Heidi doesn't look happy with Amber either, but she shrugs and puts her arm around Jen.

We play volleyball and I'm on a team with Jen and Amber. Heidi is on the other team, and the first few plays are fine. I'm feeling better than I expected to feel today, when I look over and see Jen go down. She falls on the floor and starts convulsing. The girls around her scream and I run over to see if she's okay.

"Call 911," I yell, when I get closer. Our teacher Miss Hanover runs over, calling an ambulance, and I bend down to try to keep her head from slamming against the gym floor.

"Does anyone know CPR?" I yell.

The girls look around blankly and Miss Hanover starts the compressions.

It takes five minutes before an ambulance arrives and Jen has stopped convulsing but hasn't opened her eyes. When I look up, Amber is bawling and Heidi is pacing behind Melanie and a few of the other girls. Heidi's agitated and jumpy and when Amber shoots her a hateful look, I see the fear on Heidi's face.

What is going on here?

When the paramedics come in, Miss Hanover steps aside and they rush to get Jen on a stretcher. One of the men asks a few questions.

No, she didn't seem sick before.

She didn't say anything about not feeling well.

People throw out answers left and right, and when they ask, had she taken anything? Everyone looks around and doesn't know what to say. No one answers and I wonder if anyone but Heidi knows the truth.

Luci texts me later that night and when I read it, I drop my phone.

Jen didn't make it. My parents heard it's a drug overdose. :(

I try to reach Ashton because out of all the girls at school besides me, he's closest to Jen. I remember him telling me it was hard being black in this neighborhood and that he watched out for Jen. He tried to make sure the girls treated her right. Besides the two of them and a freshman named Josiah, they're the only black kids in the school.

He doesn't answer and I eventually send him a text saying I'm worried about him and for him to call me.

He calls late that night and sounds so heavy, it breaks my heart.

"I can't believe she'd be into hard drugs. She was smarter than that," he says. "Maybe marijuana here and there, but I never saw her doing anything harder."

"I think Heidi gave her something." I tell him what I saw in gym and hear him punch something on the other end. "I'm going to talk to the principal about it tomorrow. Do you think I should go to the police?"

"No," he says. "Don't say anything yet. I don't know what's going on, but please be careful."

"I'll be okay."

"Too much has already happened to you. And I don't want to lose you too. Please, let's just wait it out a little bit? Listen around and see what we hear?"

I sigh into the phone and agree to keep my mouth shut. For now.

CHAPTER FOUR

The next day, Longlake Academy is full of tears and drama. An assembly is held during first and second period to let everyone know about Jen. I watch Heidi, Amber, and Melanie closely, as well as Henry. I haven't forgotten what I saw between any of them, even though Raf told me to forget about Henry and Heidi and whatever I saw exchanged between the two of them. I didn't tell anyone but Ashton about Heidi and Jen yesterday, and he also thought I should keep it to myself. But judging from the way Amber looks as if she's about to explode, I don't think I'll have to say a word. If Heidi is to blame, I don't think Amber will be able to stay quiet about it.

The more I think about it, the more I'm bothered that I haven't done anything about it myself before now. The whole exchange Luci and I saw after Ashton's game, with Heidi and whoever was in that car in the parking lot, was highly suspicious. *But what do I really know?* I ask myself over and over again and when I can't with a clear conscience function another second, I make my way to the office. I'm almost there when Raf steps into the hall behind me and pulls me into an empty classroom.

"What are you doing?" he asks, his face inches from mine.

"I'm going to the office."

"Why?"

"Why do you care?"

"Tell me, Gabi. I need to know."

I sigh and drag my hand down my face, exhausted with this conversation already.

"I saw something yesterday, okay? Between Heidi and Jen...Amber did too and she's upset about it."

"You need to trust me on this and stay out of it."

I feel like I'm going to explode. My temper hits hard. "How dare you tell me to stay out of it?" I poke him in the chest with every word. "Someone is dead and I think your girlfriend had something to do with it...or at least she's the one smuggling it into the school."

He assesses me coolly and knocks my finger back. "Did you see for a fact what it was? Did you get evidence? A photo, the actual drugs themselves? *Anything*?"

My eyes narrow on him and I swallow hard, backing up. He takes a step forward, moving until I hit the wall. "No, I didn't. But I think someone should know."

"Someone knows," he says.

"Who, you?"

He shifts until his nose is against mine. "Yes. Stay out of it."

"I can't believe you're willing to cover this—and for what? Because she's a sweet fuck buddy? She's not a good person, Raf. I'm so disgusted by you right now."

He smirks and his tongue reaches out and licks the seam between my lips. My heart stutters over itself. "Are you now?" His hands land on my cheeks and he kisses me hard, making my knees weak.

But I shove him away, panting. "Stop it. I want nothing to do with you."

"Right. Keep telling yourself that." He steps back in, putting his arms around my waist. "The police are questioning Heidi right now."

"They are? So you admit there's something to this?"

"I'm going to say this one more time and then I won't ever say it again because I despise broken records. I hate that you've made me become one. *Stay out of it.*"

This time when he kisses me, I sigh into his mouth and his tongue drives me crazy, sending sparks throughout my body and making me burn for him. He hikes my thigh up and thrusts into me, reminding me of the torture he stoked within me and sending the cravings into overdrive.

How can I want him so bad when I detest him this much?

Somehow I get a grasp on my dignity and push him away before he undoes my jeans, even though I want him more than my next breath.

"You don't get to do that anymore. We're nothing," I tell him. I can't say that and look him in the eye though, and when he lifts my chin up, I close my eyes.

"Look at me."

"No," I whisper.

"You need reminding..."

"Of what?"

"That you're mine."

I laugh and it sounds deranged. "You can't make up your mind enough to know who you are, let alone who you own...which is *not* me, by the way. No one will *ever* own me."

He chuckles and my eyes open, ready to kick him if he laughs at me again. "You're so cute when you're in denial."

I slam my foot down on his and he yelps, backing up and dropping his hands long enough for me to skirt past him.

"This isn't over," he says as I leave the room.

"Oh, it never began. Don't forget that, Raf. We don't have anything to continue, so just leave me alone. You've been acting like I'm invisible since—" I leave it hanging and swallow hard, the memory of the water just out of reach. "Stay out of my way. And if you know something about Jen, for God's sake, do the right thing and get your dick out of the way. Heidi Serrin is not worth it."

"Your kiss says we're everything. Your eyes. We're something, at least in *your* mind." He walks toward me, his lips swollen from our kiss. "We'll never be *nothing*."

I get out of there before he can touch me again. Because he's right. When he touches me, I lose control and the truth of my feelings comes out.

But what I *need* and what is the *truth* are not the same things.

It sucks that I have to ride home with Raf after my run-in with him, but thankfully, Ashton is with us. Luci got another ride. Ashton says he can walk home from our house, but Raf ignores him and drops him off in front of his place. I roll my eyes at Raf and lean over the seat to hug Ashton. Raf says something snarky under his breath, but we both ignore him.

Neither of us speak on the drive to our houses. It's a few blocks, but it feels like miles. When we pull onto our street,

I gasp when I see a few police cars on the sidewalk in front of my house.

"Not this again."

"Maybe they just have a few questions. Try not to freak out until we know what's happening." Raf tries to be reassuring, but I'm already running down the driveway. I stumble into the house and my mom is sitting across from three police officers, with Stefen by her side.

She walks over and hugs me when she sees the terror on my face.

"There were more lilies," she says.

I swallow hard and nod, sitting on the loveseat closest to her. Raf sits next to me and as much as I hate to find it comforting, it is.

"Would you mind if we asked your daughter a few questions?" one of the officers asks.

"If she's comfortable answering, sure," Mom says.

"I'm Officer Bramsford. Do you mind? It won't take long." He seems to be the one in charge and he smiles kindly, trying to set me at ease.

"I'll do my best."

"Can you tell us the significance of the red lilies?"

"My...uh, Luke...he used to give me one every time we..." I turn to my mom. "I'm not comfortable answering this here."

Stefen stands up and motions for Raf to leave with him. "We'll be back as soon as you need us," he tells my mom. Raf gives me a strange look as he walks out, but he's the last person I want listening while I discuss Luke.

I'd rather my mom not be here for this either, but I'm too tired for the fight that would bring.

When Stefen and Raf are outside, I turn back to Officer Bramsford. "Luke gave me a lily almost every time we saw each other. All but the first time we met. I was given one or more every time I had sex with him. He'd leave them for me when he wanted to see me and one when I'd go to his house. It'd be on the bed when I got there."

"And what do you think this means now? Do you have a place to meet?"

"No," I say sharply. I look at my mom to make sure she doesn't think that either. "Not here. I was only ever with him in Vegas. I thought I saw him once here, when I was out with a friend, but I haven't talked to him, and I'm not even sure that was him." I hesitate before I continue. "I've gotten the lilies at school too."

"What?" my mom gasps.

"So others know about the flowers?"

"Just my mother...oh, and Ashton. He doesn't know who they're from, he's just seen them. And my friend Luci saw the one I got in my locker."

My mom shakes her head. "I haven't told anyone."

"And this Ashton, is he a friend of yours? Do you trust him?"

"I trust him completely." I try to imagine all the times he's seen the flowers. He seemed just as shaken as I was the last time. He wasn't nervous because he had something to do with it, was he? *No, that's crazy. Stop.* "I trust Luci too."

I jump when Officer Bramsford speaks again. "Has anything else unusual been going on?"

"I've felt like I'm being watched, but no...except when I was hit on the back of the head."

"Right. And did you see anyone then?"

"No."

"Okay, if you think of anything else, will you let us know. Anything at all, even if you don't think it's important."

"Sure. *Is* he in town? And has he made some kind of deal with the police or something?"

"I'm not sure what you're asking, but we're not personally working with him, no. And he's not supposed to be within three hundred feet of you, so if you see him, call us right away. We'll make sure he stays away."

"Okay. Thank you."

They leave shortly after that and I think of so many other questions I should've asked. If we catch him putting the flowers on my doorstep, can he get arrested? Do they know where he is now?

They didn't tell me anything.

Every day has more questions than answers.

Why haven't they found my dad or Luke by now? Why haven't we caught them sneaking onto our property? And while I had them, I regret not bringing up Jen and the drugs at my school. I wish I'd said something, even though the two are completely unrelated.

I'm letting Jen down by keeping quiet.

CHAPTER FIVE

On Friday night, my mom comes dancing into my room. "Come on, get dressed. We're going to a party."

She's got on a cute maxi dress with a jean jacket and she pulls me by the hand until I'm standing.

"No...I don't feel like going anywhere. Isn't it kind of late for that anyway?"

"It's not even nine yet."

"It seems like a weird time for a party. A girl from school *died* this week, Mom."

"All the more reason to embrace life more, sweetie."

I frown. "It just feels wrong."

"You've spent the majority of your time here doing schoolwork. You hardly go anywhere. Put on something cute. Come on, you're acting like the old lady here. Live a little. It's been way too morose around here for...months, not just now. Let me do your makeup. Your hair already looks great. You're like a young Megan Fox, anyone ever tell you that? Is she still a thing?"

"No—I don't know. I haven't seen her in anything in a long time. My hair's lighter than hers."

My mom makes an exasperated sound with her mouth and motions for me to hurry up and let her work her magic. I groan.

At school, they're too busy putting ketchup and porn pictures of my mom in my locker to compliment me in any way. It's on the tip of my tongue to tell her no one would ever compare me to someone pretty, but I don't say it. She's trying to be sweet and I need to stop shutting her down. This has been a stressful year for her too—I'm not the only one suffering after this move. And the years of stress she endured alone—before getting to her breaking point with my dad—I owe her so much for being brave enough to leave.

I wish she'd been brave so much sooner, but...

Stop. Give her a chance.

She looks so hopeful. She pulls out a cute sweater and my best jeans.

"No dress for me? I'm surprised." I grin and she lifts a shoulder, laughing.

"I didn't want to push my luck."

"Let me wash up. I won't get my hair wet in the shower."

"Hurry."

"What is your deal?"

She shrugs again and I give her a deadpan stare until she laughs harder.

I take the world's fastest shower and when I get out, I take my hair out of the clip and give it a shake. I lotion up and put on the jeans and sweater she laid out on the bathroom counter, opening the door to let the mirror clear so she can do my makeup.

I sit on the counter and she bites her lower lip as she applies my makeup. When she's done, she steps back and admires her work, her cheeks lifting with her huge smile.

"Perfect."

"Where are we going?"

"You'll see."

She has me turn toward the mirror and my eyes widen as I take in what she's done. She's used less than I usually do, but it looks a thousand times better. My eyes shine like blue sapphires and my lips are plump and kissable. My skin is flawless and I reach up to touch my lashes. I don't know how she's made them look fuller with less mascara, but she has.

"Look how your eyes pop."

"Thanks, Mom."

"You're welcome. Now, let's go. I have it on good authority that the hot dogs won't last long."

"Hot dogs?" I crinkle my nose in disgust and she laughs.

"I know, not your favorite. But how long since you've eaten one?"

"Uh, when I was four?"

"Exactly. Time to try again."

"Yuck." I'm still griping about it when we walk out the door. I'm walking toward the car when she grabs my arm.

"This way," she says, leading me out of the gate and toward the beach behind us.

I can hear laughter nearby and the closer we get, the more crowded it becomes. What I'd started to hope was a private little bonfire with my mom and maybe Ashton's family sounds like something entirely different. I start to ask her about Mrs. Cromwell and if they've worked things out yet, but I'm distracted by all the people.

"What's going on?" I look at her suspiciously.

"Just a little party," she says as we step onto the sand and into the twinkle lights of a huge gathering behind Raf's house. There's a massive bonfire and music playing. A long table with food and drinks sits to the side and there are people everywhere. I look around for Ashton and Luci, but I don't spot them. A few couples are dancing and when Stefen sees us, he comes over right away.

"Ladies, you are both especially lovely this evening," he says. His eyes roam over my mother and she shivers, flushing as she takes his hand.

I cringe, but it's kind of sweet, I guess. He walks away with her and I'm left standing alone, trying to see if any of these people are ones who have ever been nice to me or...

Yeah, there's Heidi.

Nope, I don't think I want to do this tonight. Pretty certain I don't.

I turn around to go home and walk straight into Raf.

"Party's the other way."

"I think I've had enough, thanks."

"You haven't even eaten yet." He holds up a big hot dog covered with all kinds of color that can't be natural for food. "Here, have mine."

"No, thank you. Not into that."

He looks at me like I'm crazy. "Really? Or did they just tell you that in Vegas?"

"Both."

"Ha, what I thought. Try it. I dare you."

I glare at him and my shoulders sag. Of course he knows I can't resist a dare. I open my mouth and he puts the hot dog in my mouth, his eyes gleaming. It's a huge bite, but when I start chewing, the burst of flavors—as much as I hate to admit it—it's *delicious*. I close my eyes so I don't have to see the triumph on his face. And I savor my massive bite.

"Fuck. That's hot. Here, have some more."

He nudges the hot dog to my mouth again and I open my

mouth. This time, I watch him while I chew. He's staring at me with such lust I feel like I need to take a cold shower. He feeds the rest of it to me and when I eat the last bite, I'm sorry it's gone.

"Would you like another? I'll make you one."

My cheeks feel hot and like I've just experienced a long round of foreplay. "Uh, no, thank you. It was good though, you were right."

He tilts his head and grins. "What did you say?" He tugs on his ear. "Did you just admit that I was right about something?"

I bite on the inside of my cheek, my grin still getting too big. "So when did this party come about?"

"Raf!" Heidi's whiny voice screeches behind me and I watch his expression change from heated to blank.

I turn and she's walking over, pulling her sweatshirt over her head and revealing a bikini top. The bonfire is putting out heat but not enough for a swimsuit.

I notice Ashton and Henry walking onto the beach then and a cheer goes up. They must have won tonight's football game. I'm the worst friend—I forgot all about his game. I wave, moving past Raf. His fingers brush against my arm like he's trying to stop me, but I hurry away from him, eager to get away from the heat he's projecting.

I hug Ashton and say hello to Henry. He's looking past me to Heidi and Raf, his mouth tightening in...what? Jealousy? I turn just as Heidi jumps into Raf's arms. He catches her like it's nothing and when she starts kissing him, we all stare at them. He turns and his eyes are open as they kiss. He stares right through me, never blinking, as they tangle tongues.

My eyes blur and I turn away before he sees me looking as desolate as I feel. Henry stalks off and I stagger into

Ashton. He holds my head against his chest, lowering his lips to my hair.

He whispers, "Do you wanna get out of here?"

I lean back and look at him as a tear falls back into my hair. "I can't leave yet. It'll seem like I care."

"But you do. Why not show how you feel?"

"Because he would just find another way to hurt me with it."

"Then he does not deserve your happiness or your sadness."

He leans down and kisses me, his lips tentative at first and then when his tongue meets mine, I'm surprised at how incredible it feels. His fingers wind through my hair and his body presses tight against mine, allowing me to feel every contour of his shape, even the way he gets hard against me.

"Ashton?" I whisper when we pull apart.

He grins down at me, his forehead touching mine. "I've wanted to do that for a long time now."

"I thought—"

"I did too, but that felt amazing, didn't it?"

"Yes, but..."

He laughs and puts his hands on my cheeks. "I know you're hung up on Raf, don't worry. But damn, our lips work well together."

I giggle against his mouth, my earlier tears forgotten. "Yeah. Weird."

He grabs my hand and we walk past Heidi and Raf. Heidi's hands are on Raf's chest and he's got his hands in his hair, looking like he's going to kill someone. His eyes are ice and I don't let my gaze stay on his for long, too keen on letting him think I'm completely unaffected by him. I'm shaky even after I'm far past him, but I don't know if it's because of him or Ashton's kiss.

I lace my fingers through Ashton's and we start running toward the water. I take off my shoes at the last second and when our toes hit the water, I squeal and take off running.

It doesn't hit me until later that I was near water again and I didn't want it to take me under.

CHAPTER SIX

Raf: What the fuck was that on the beach?

I stare at my phone. It's almost midnight and I left the party almost half an hour ago. I told my mom I was heading back to the house and she stayed out at the bonfire with Stefen. Ashton walked me to the door and he didn't repeat the kiss, so I'm not sure if that was entirely for Raf's benefit or what. He did give me the biggest hug and said he'd call me tomorrow, so maybe we'll talk about it then.

I think of a dozen different ways I could respond to Raf's text, but I'm so annoyed by it, especially after he had Heidi, the bitchy druggie, straddled around his waist, kissing her. He has no right to demand any answers from me. I don't owe him anything, especially when I have no idea myself what the fuck that was.

I'm smiling when I fall asleep though. The beauty of the kiss in itself was liberating...but also the justice of it. I decide not to overthink it and just be happy that it happened, for whatever reason. It made me feel better and it made Raf miserable.

Two things I can feel good about.

When I wake up the next morning, I pick up my phone. Ten o'clock. Can't remember the last time I slept this late.

There are three more messages from Raf.

Raf: *Answer me, dammit*.

Raf: *Fuck, Gabi. What are you trying to prove? You know fucking well you don't belong with Ashton*.

Those were sent at two this morning, so I'm guessing he didn't sleep as well as I did.

Raf: *We need to talk*.

That one was sent at seven.

I'd feel sorry for him if he wasn't such a jerk.

———

My mom comes floating into the kitchen while I'm eating cereal. Stefen isn't far behind her. I lift an eyebrow at her and she flushes.

"Oh, we're having sleepovers now?"

"No." She presses her lips firmly together. "He came by while you were still asleep. Don't be like that, Jo-Gab..." she stutters. "How did you sleep?"

"Better than you, apparently."

I still don't know how I feel about my mom dating Stefen. I don't trust the guy. I'd like my mom to be happy, but there are too many loose ends hanging with Stefen that he won't answer. The problem is, my mom's not giving me any answers either. I need to find out what they know about Luke and they're keeping me in the dark.

I force a smile at her and she relaxes slightly, getting eggs out of the refrigerator.

"Would you like some breakfast, Stefen?"

"Sure." He grins.

"Gabi?"

I hold my spoon up. "I'm fine. Thanks, though." I drink the last of the milk in my bowl and take it to the sink.

"You're not rushing off, are you? Sit with us for a while."

"I need to get started on homework."

"Okay." She pouts, but when I walk down the hall, Stefen says something and she laughs so hard, I know she's okay.

For now.

I hope he doesn't hurt her.

I'm still in sweats and a tank top when my mom yells up the stairs that I have company. I throw a sweatshirt over my tank and check my messy bun. It's not my best look, but it'll have to do.

I walk downstairs and Raf is standing there looking like broody sex. I scowl at him and he scowls back. It's torture every time I see him. I don't exactly regret having sex with him because the experience was out of this world, but it's painful, knowing I can't go there again. I feel a trickle of sweat form near my hairline and brush it away.

He does not affect me.

I hear him in my head saying, *"Right. Keep telling yourself that."*

"What are you doing here?" I ask.

"Seemed like your phone wasn't working." He crosses his arms over his chest and I do the same.

"It's working fine. I didn't like your tone."

Stefen clears his throat and we both turn toward him. "This little—whatever it is between the two of you—it needs to get resolved right away because I don't need it getting between Sarah and me."

Raf stiffens next to me and I want to light into Stefen. *How dare he?* I decide to let Raf do all the talking for both of us once he starts. It doesn't take long to know we're on the same page about this at least.

"Gabi and I are completely separate from you and whatever this is you have going on with Sarah. It's none of your business." He holds up his hand when Stefen starts to respond and Stefen's mouth closes. "And since you didn't ask for our input when you started screwing each other, or even tell us it was going on until long after the fact, you don't get to give your input into how we talk to one another. Got it?"

If I talked to my dad like that, I would be black and blue for a week, but whatever Raf has over his dad or whatever arrangement they have in their relationship is a different story. Stefen blinks and then gives a barely noticeable nod.

"Treat each other with respect. That's all I ask," he says, his tone much quieter this time.

I watch as Raf stares his dad down. Then they clasp hands and do a weird handshake, and I wonder what it would be like to have a peaceful relationship with my father. It's not something I've ever known or considered.

But then right before I leave the room, I hear Stefen say under his breath, "Keep your hands off of her, Raf. You touch her, and I'll make your life a living hell. Take that input and stick it where it belongs."

Too late, I want to shout at his father.

I don't wait around to hear what Raf says back. My mom walks in as he's saying that and chuckles the way she does when she's uncomfortable. I cringe. I think back to her excitement when she first thought Raf was a boyfriend possibility—how quickly she changed her mind when she realized he was Stefen's son.

It's unsettling how similar Raf sounds to his father. Now I know where he gets it.

What does this mean for my mom?

Raf follows me to my bedroom, despite me telling him I don't want to talk to him. He nudges me in the back and I keep going up the stairs. When I reach the top, I turn toward him before we step inside my bedroom.

"Say it out here."

He motions to my room. "I want to say it in there."

"No."

"Please?"

My mouth drops, the shock too real for me to hide. "Don't think I've ever heard you say *please* before."

His eyes start smiling before his lips do and I study the transformation in his face like a girl seeing snow or the beach for the first time. Complete awe and wonder. I quickly school my features and fold my arms across my chest.

"You better make it quick or our parents will wonder what we're up to."

He lifts an eyebrow. "You think I care what they think? Let their imaginations run wild for all I fucking care."

I bite my lower lip, unsure how to respond to that. "Your dad sounds—"

"Forget about him."

The doorbell rings and my mom answers it. When I hear Ashton's voice and see Raf's expression fall, I know I should try to figure out the best way to handle this, but life is too complicated to worry about every little thing.

I yell. "We're up here."

Raf's eyes narrow, fiery, as he cages me in with his arms. "What game are you playing, pretty girl?"

My heart softens the slightest bit with his endearment, but I hear Ashton and glance under Raf's arm to grin and say hello.

"No games," I tell Raf. "No games," I say to Ashton.

He grins back. Raf doesn't.

I duck underneath his arm and stand next to Raf as Ashton reaches the top stair.

"Came to see if you want to go to the new coffee shop," Ashton says. "But I can see you're—"

"Sure, I'd love to. Let me just get a jacket."

Raf steps in the room behind me and stops me, tugging on my sleeve. "If you leave with him, Gabi, I won't be here when you get back. I mean, I won't be—"

"Why don't you come with us?"

He stares at me like that's beyond his comprehension. For a second, there's hope and then it's gone. He bites his bottom lip and then shakes his head.

"Suit yourself."

I walk past him and Ashton moves into the doorway.

"Raf? Wanna come too?" he asks.

Raf drags his hand through his hair and looks tormented for a second. Then I think I've imagined it all because his expression returns to stone.

"Nah. I'm good. Have fun."

He stalks out of the room, pounding down the stairs, and he's out the door before I have even reached my doorway.

"What was that?"

"Who knows?" I say.

But my heart worries that Raf just turned something off that he might not ever reopen. For one brief second, I thought he might show me who he is and be willing to bend even the tiniest crack. But as quickly as I saw the window open, he slammed it shut.

Ashton and I drive to the new coffee shop, not saying much on the way. I order a chai latte and he orders a mocha and we sit at the table near the back window. A fireplace is roaring and I look around, smiling at the cute decor. When I taste my latte, I start nodding.

"Oh yeah, they'll do well. It's delicious."

"You approve?"

"Wholeheartedly."

He grins and tries his mocha, his eyes narrowing in agreement. "Yes."

"Are we going to talk about the bonfire?"

"The kiss of all kisses?" He lifts his mug over his mouth until I only see his twinkling eyes.

I snort. "Well, when you put it that way..."

"Do we need to talk about it? It was fucking hot, that's all I know," he says.

"I'm just tired of all the back and forth with Raf...and not wanting to get into something complicated with you. What we have is so nice and easy...and has felt platonic."

"I don't think I've made it a secret that I like you."

"Well, kind of—but not in that way. I didn't...know exactly," I stutter to get it out. "You like Raf?"

"And I like you." He shrugs. "Raf and me—we're never going to happen. I'm letting that go. But I know you like him. I also know we're going our separate ways to school next fall. You're aiming for Columbia and I'm counting on the University of Alabama." He leans in and sets his mug down. "But you're not going to lose my friendship, ever. If you need me for anything, and I mean, *anything*," he laughs, "I'm here."

My eyes widen as I hear what he's saying and what he's *not* saying.

"The look on Raf's face after I kissed you. Priceless," he says. "If you want nothing to do with me from here on out, I'd like to think I helped your cause with that kiss. And it was fucking *hot*."

I lean my head over on the table, hiding it in my arms as I laugh until I cry. When I come up for air, he's laughing too and I wipe my eyes. "I don't even know what to say. You might be the best thing to ever happen to me. I never want to lose your friendship either. Let's just plan on not letting that happen, okay?" I take a sip of my drink just to calm down. "But we should probably not make a habit of kissing like that often because it could get...confusing."

"Fair enough. Unless we want to explore how much hotter we can take this." He presses his lips together and we lose it again, laughing until my chest hurts.

I hold my hand and shake my head, trying to catch my breath. "Friends. We're *friends*."

We laugh again, but he nods and clinks my mug with his.

We make a stop at the bookstore and then head back home. Raf is nowhere to be found when we pull in, and I don't even want to think about what I'll deal with the next time I see him. But at least with Ashton, I think we're good. It's nice to have one thing in my life going right.

CHAPTER SEVEN

The rest of the weekend is quiet. Dangerously so, because it makes me think of Raf too much. He was actually being sweet at the party and then that kiss between him and Heidi...it did a number on me. Once again, he managed to flip everything upside down and make me feel like an idiot... and then had the nerve to get mad at me for kissing Ashton.

It's infuriating that as nice as that kiss was with Ashton, Raf is still the one that has my heart all tangled up in knots.

On Sunday morning, before I'm fully awake, my mom barrels into my room.

I stare at her, shifting my crazy hair out of my eyes. "It's Sunday. What are you doing?" I put my pillow over my head and groan. It took me forever to fall asleep.

"Why did you try to fool me into believing Ashton is gay?" she demands.

I lift the pillow and stare at her. She's grinning and tapping her foot like she can't contain her excitement. I'm actually impressed she managed to hold off until now to ask me this.

"Because it's *true*."

"That kiss Friday night was no joke," she says. "Someone *gay* does not kiss a girl like that."

"Times have changed, Mom. It was a nice kiss. I still don't think it means we're a couple."

"But maybe?"

I sigh and pile two pillows on top of my head, waving for her to go away.

She giggles and closes my door, but not before shouting, "He is so cute. And that kiss. Wow!"

I groan. How does a porn star end up starry-eyed about romance?

By Sunday night, I'm sick of thinking about Raf, sick of wondering what's going to happen next with Luke, worrying about what Ashton feels...and the worst—I can't stop wondering where my dad is.

I'm all over the place.

I can't think about my dad too much or I go crazy. There are too many reasons why it's best that we are far apart. Across the country isn't far enough, and I don't know why I ever believed he would keep his word about anything.

It hurts too much. The thought that he's behind the video...if that's even true. What kind of a father would be okay exposing his daughter like that to the world?

One that was okay with his wife being exploited for years.

Yes, my mom initially made the choice to be a porn star, but she wanted out long before he ever allowed her to get out. And I thought the whole thing between Luke and me was what forced my father's hand...why he let us go.

Did he really just use that to hurt us more? Nothing about that makes sense to me. I don't understand how a father could be capable of that...but what do I know about fathers other than the one I've had? I don't know my grandparents. Both parents have always stayed quiet about their lives growing up, but I know they didn't have very loving relationships with their families, even before they worked in the porn industry. I used to try to get information out of my mom about her family because it felt like we were an island. I longed to have a connection with someone other than our little family unit.

I never got much out of her...only that the hurts were deep and that neither side wanted anything to do with the other.

I set my book aside and stare out the window, movement next door catching my eye. I can only see the side portion of their yard and Raf is jogging up to the house. He tugs his shirt off and wipes his face. I duck when he glances up, hoping he can't see me from this distance.

I've been gun-shy about friendships, never had the normal school development that I should've gotten from day one, so I have no idea how much this weirdness is my fault and how much of it is a crazy situation that wouldn't be the typical for anyone. I guess I'll never know since I only have my experiences or lack thereof to go on. But it would be nice to feel like I know what I'm doing. Maybe life is this complicated for everyone, or maybe the curses my parents have carried with them are passing down to me and I'll pass them on to my children and their children.

God, that's depressing. I need to get out of this house.

I chance another look outside and Raf is gone. I want to go for a run down the beach, but I feel like a prisoner stuck in this house. Until something is resolved and these lilies stop showing up at random times, I'm scared to go anywhere alone.

At least tonight.

Maybe tomorrow I'll get my bravery back.

Heidi's kiss with Raf gave her all kinds of bravado because at school on Monday, she's hanging all over him like a ratty shirt. He stares at me woodenly and doesn't do anything to remove her hands from his body.

It makes me sick.

Her desperation makes me sick, and his acceptance of her makes me even sicker.

For someone who's just lost a friend, she sure doesn't seem torn up about it.

His words play over and over in my head about staying out of the mystery with Jen's death and the longer I think about it, the more I know I can't sit by and say nothing. Regardless of what he seems to think, he does not dictate what I do with my life. Ashton doesn't either, for that matter. I square my shoulders and get a backbone. I think all of this with my mom's assault and mine...I haven't known which end is up.

But enough is enough.

During lunch, I go to the office and ask to speak to Principal Saunders. I wait for about twenty minutes while he's finishing his lunch and then he calls me in.

We've had little interaction with each other, but he seems off today. Maybe it's the fact that a student recently died while under his care.

"What can I do for you, Ms. Sinclair?"

"I don't know if this will help, but I wanted to tell you about something I saw between Jen Ames and Heidi Serrin."

His lips purse tighter and he nods down at his desk. "Okay."

"I saw Heidi give Jen a bag of something that looked like

drugs. I thought at the time it was coke, but I'm not one hundred percent it was that—it could've been another drug."

"How close were you?"

"Uh...close enough to see that it was drugs?"

"But not to be sure about what it was?"

"Like I said, not one hundred percent, but I'm not fully educated on what every drug looks like either."

"Did you see Jen take the substance?"

"No, but..."

"Would it be safe to say that it's taken some time for you to adjust to the school environment at Longlake?"

I clamp my mouth shut, feeling my frustration rise that this is the way the conversation is going. He's making me feel like I'm being paranoid and intrusive.

"I don't know what that has to do with anything—I think I'm adjusting fine given what I've dealt with since being here."

"I'm not sure what you mean by that and I'm not insinuating anything other than perhaps you're misreading the situation. Do you have a lot of experience with substances, Gabriela?"

My eyes widen and I stand up, causing my chair to almost fall back. I grab it before it crashes on the floor.

"No, I don't have a lot of experience with *drugs*. Do you?" His jaw ticks and it doesn't take a brain to know he wants me out of here. "I know enough to say I'm pretty sure she took something and passed out right after. I heard later that it was a drug overdose. I don't know why you wouldn't want to know that it could be because of drugs on your campus. I've seen girls using in the bathroom before, also usually in Heidi's possession, and I think since one of your students has died, you might want to know where it's getting in."

"I don't like to operate under assumptions. If you can get solid evidence for me, I will consider it. Thank you for coming forward, I'll be sure to take note of your thoughts on this."

I'm at the door already, mortified by his nonchalance and so unbelievably angry. He obviously wants to sweep all of this under the rug and claim no wrongdoing whatsoever on the part of the school.

"Hopefully no one else dies on your watch," I say before I leave his office.

He grabs my shoulder before I can leave, holding me in place.

"I don't deal well with threats, Ms. Sinclair. I've taken your thoughts into consideration and I suggest you stick to letting the police do their job. A student's life is no small matter. I hope you're not suggesting that I played a part in anyone dying at Longlake."

I brush his hand off of my shoulder and his face flushes a little under my scrutiny. "I wasn't suggesting anything before I came in here, but now you have me questioning *everything*."

I get out of there and try to keep my head down the rest of the day. I do my work and stay out of Raf and Heidi's way. For the most part, it works. After school, Ashton finds me before he goes to practice.

"Our last game is this Friday night. Will you put it on your schedule?" He says it like he's joking, but I can see the eagerness in his eyes.

"Sure. I'll be there."

"Great. I've gotta get to practice. I've hardly seen you today. You okay?"

"Yeah, I'm fine.

"Okay." He gives me another look before waving over his shoulder. I want to run after him and tell him what happened with Mr. Saunders, but he's rushing off to practice.

I turn and Raf is watching me. Angry. *Of course*. His constant anger with me is exhausting. My shoulders sag and I turn toward my locker. I can't win. I wish we could settle into something...*anything* other than this. I don't expect to be friends with him, but something less hostile would be nice. I shut my locker door and hurry past him, ready to be home.

I feel him watching me as I walk down the hall and then Heidi steps out of the bathroom near the exit, her pupils dilated. She laughs her high-pitched giggle that sends chills down my spine, it's so grating, and I keep walking.

"Raf," she calls. She bumps into me when she says it and laughs harder. "Watch where you're going, slut."

I reach out and drive my fist into her nose, not stopping when she screams and falls back against the locker.

"You bitch!" she wails. "Did you break my nose? She broke my nose! What the fuck!"

She yanks my hair and I pull my fist back, ready to hit her again as she flails around, eyes crazed.

"Get your hands off of me. If your nose isn't broken now, I can make sure it is with the next punch."

Her eyes widen into something comical and she lets go of my hair, clutching her nose and crying so hard her shoulders shake.

I keep walking until I'm out the door.

If someone can die at Longlake, what's a little broken nose going to cost me?

Whatever it is will be worth it.

CHAPTER EIGHT

Turns out it'll cost me a week's suspension.

But it shouldn't affect my transcripts because I'm a stellar student.

That's what Mr. Saunders tells my mother as I stare at him stonily across the desk.

I have a feeling my time with him earlier today is both helping and hurting my cause at the moment.

I feel bad for my mom. She keeps looking at me like she doesn't know what devil has occupied her daughter's body, and I'm not making it any easier on her because I won't tell her anything that happened. I just want out of this office and to get as far from Longlake as possible.

"This won't happen again, I can assure you of that," she says to Mr. Saunders as he opens the office door.

"Don't make promises you can't keep, Mom," I say under my breath.

She jabs me in the side and I keep my mouth shut.

"Make sure that it doesn't." Mr. Saunders clears his throat. "We have a no-tolerance stance on bullying here at Longlake."

I throw my head back and laugh hysterically at that and then my mom really does look at me like I've lost my mind.

I stand up and turn to both of them, hands on my hips. "I've been bullied since the day I got here and haven't *once* been saved from anyone, teachers *or* students. I'd say it's *more* than *tolerated* all over this school. Heidi Serrin had it coming, trust me. And no, I don't plan on hitting her again, but if she calls me a *slut* one more time and gives drugs to another nice person and they *wind up dead*, yeah, I might have to hit her again. Since no one else is doing anything about it!" I'm yelling now and the few students and teachers lingering around the office are staring through the windows and open door, listening to every word of my breakdown.

My mom yanks my arm and drags me out of the office. "Shut your mouth," she says between gritted teeth.

I recognize one of the boys from the day my video was circulating, standing there with his mouth gaping. I give him the finger and he grins as my mom huffs again, pulling me farther down the hall. When we get outside, she still doesn't let go of my arm and I dread the car ride home.

I was right to dread it because she doesn't stop ranting the whole way home. I tune her out as she tells me all the reasons what I did was so destructive and poor behavior and evil and asking for trouble and bad attention and blah de blah de blah.

She turns to face me when she stops the car in front of our house. "Since you don't do anything, I don't even know what to take away to punish you. How could you do this to me, Jocelyn? You know we're trying so hard to create a new beginning."

"Did you not hear what I said in the office? A student *died* and I wasn't even really friends with her, but I seem to be the only one who cares that she's dead. What's wrong with everyone else? I didn't do any of this to *you*. I hit Heidi Serrin because she had it coming. I'm tired of no one paying for their bad behavior. Ever. Except me, of course." I laugh again. I laugh until my stomach hurts and the tears are dripping down my cheeks. "Did you even hear me saying I've been bullied since I got to that school? What part of that makes it payback to *you*?"

"Doesn't look like you're being bullied now." She shakes her head and slams the door to the car and then the door to the house. I sit in the car for a long time, contemplating how I'll function without school for a week.

Sounds like heaven.

Maybe I should've punched Heidi sooner.

Ashton stops by later and I hear my mom telling him that I'm grounded. She took my phone when I walked into the house; I wasn't even allowed to let Luci or Ashton know what was going on. I can tell he's turning on the charm when she laughs, but I also hear her telling him no, she's not making exceptions, even for him.

The game Friday night. Ugh. Hopefully I can talk her into letting me out of the house before then.

I haven't had anything to care about until now. And it feels kind of nice to know Luci and Ashton will miss me.

I read a book and stay up late, not worrying about getting up early the next morning. I'm drifting off when I hear something against my window and I try to look without being seen.

Raf stands outside and I watch as he bends down and throws a little rock at the window. When he does it a third time, I grab a jacket and put it on over my tank and sweats. I tiptoe down the stairs, making sure my mom isn't hiding behind any corners.

All is quiet.

I shut the door behind me, walking around to where Raf is waiting.

"Your mom is at my house," he says.

"Oh, I didn't hear her leave."

"Thought you might like to get out of the house while you have a chance."

"Thanks."

He shrugs.

The sounds of the nearby water and birds still squawking here and there help fill the awkward moment while we avoid looking at each other.

"So...you're out of school for the week," he says.

"Yeah."

"Good."

"What's that supposed to mean?"

He sighs and stares at the sky like my presence is sheer torture.

"Hey, you're the one who got me down here in the middle of the night, the least you can do is have a real conversation."

"It's eleven o'clock."

My eyes narrow on him as I lift both hands in annoyance. "Excuse me, not the middle of the night."

He lifts a shoulder and smirks.

"What are you doing here, Raf?"

"I...don't know." He puts his hands in his pockets. "Want to walk down the beach until we're tired?"

"I should stay close to home until my mom comes back."

"You know she stays until at least two when she comes over, right?"

"Uh, no. I didn't know that. I didn't know she was leaving at all." I shiver and tighten my jacket around me.

"Yeah." His voice is husky and it sends another shiver through me.

It's these times when Raf is...softer...that are the most confusing. Anything seems possible when he's like this, and that's when he's the most dangerous of all.

"I guess I could walk a little while. Don't have to get up early in the morning." I laugh and in the moonlight, I can see his lips slightly lift in a smile. "You do though."

"I don't sleep much."

He motions for me to follow him and we walk out the back gate and turn away from both of our houses. The night is brisk and the water sounds turbulent, like a storm is blowing in. We didn't get many storms in Vegas, and I'm excited by the thought of one here. The times it's rained have been a whole new experience.

"Do you do this a lot? Walk out here at night?"

"More in the warmer months, but even when it gets colder than this...yeah, I guess I do spend a lot of time out here. I like how no one is out this late. And the way the sky looks...it's peaceful. I feel less...alone."

My heart skips ahead a little and I glance at Raf. His face is hard to read in this light, but his shadow casts a foreboding spell compared to his words.

"Do you feel alone a lot?" I ask quietly.

"Yes. Don't you?" He looks at me then and grabs me when I stumble on a rock or shell. Heat spreads throughout my body, as it does every time he touches me, and my breath catches in my chest.

"Yes, I do." It's freeing to admit it. And it's intoxicating the way his hand drags down my arm and takes hold of my hand. I don't know what's going on right now, but I don't want to break the spell.

Our fingers fit together like they were made for each other and I feel the tingles from that slight contact more than I should.

"What else do you do to pass the time when you aren't sleeping?"

"I play my guitar, write songs...usually out here too because it's something my dad isn't too happy about."

"Why would he mind if you write songs?"

"He thinks anything I do to pursue music is a huge waste of time."

I stare up at him, shocked that he's opening up to me like this. And who knew he'd have such interesting things to say? Maybe I just think everything about him is interesting.

"It's what I want more than anything, but it'll never happen."

"You love it?" I ask, already assuming he does.

"Yeah," he says softly. "It's one of the only things I'm good at...besides sex," he adds, laughing.

The tension between us builds until I can hardly breathe. We reach a place on the sand where it gets rocky and stop walking. He looks down at me and steps closer, pushing back the hair blowing in my face. His other hand lands on my waist and his lips are on mine in the next second. His full lips are soft and cushiony and then demanding, as his tongue dances against mine. He tugs me against him and I stand on my tiptoes, my body aching to meld into every part of him. We kiss and kiss and kiss, until I'm breathless, my heart racing against his. He lowers me onto the sand and kisses down my chest, his tongue tracing circles against my skin as he slides my shirt to the side.

When it latches around my nipple, my back arches into him and he groans.

"Raf," I moan.

My voice unleashes something in him. He lifts up and his eyes drill mine, as if asking permission. I bite my lower lip and put my hands on his cheeks pulling him against my mouth again.

It's all the permission he needs.

He drags my sweats down and lowers his mouth to my skin, groaning when I arch into him.

"I've missed your taste so much," he whispers, before diving back inside with his tongue.

"I want you," I whimper. "Please."

"I didn't bring a condom," he says. "Oh...wait...maybe in my wallet." He digs in his pocket, pulling his wallet out and laughs when he finds one. "Goddamn, it's our night."

I'm so scared of something ruining the moment but am so hungry for him, I grab it from him and unwrap it, holding it up as he pulls his pants down. When his cock springs free, I wrap him up and he groans when my hands close around him.

"I might not last," he whispers. "It's been too long."

I stare at him, wondering if he's been with anyone since we were together. But I let all thoughts of that go when he buries himself inside of me. My eyes roll back in my head and I don't care that we're on the sand and it's messy and chilly and if anyone were to be on the beach right now, they'd totally see us.

"You feel so good," I moan. I clench around him and he curses.

"Hold still, baby."

My eyes widen and so do his as we stare at one another. And then he starts to move. He fucks me inside out and sideways. The waves swallow up our cries as we throw all caution to the wind and let our bodies worship each other without trying to figure out why we can't seem to stop this.

When our tremors still, he pulls out and takes care of the condom, tying it and throwing it in a nearby garbage. By the time he's back, I have my pants back in place, cringing at all the sand. He looks at me tentatively and holds out his hand, helping me up. We don't say anything on the walk back to the house and when we reach my house, he stops and puts his hands in his pockets.

"Sleep well," he says, his voice raspier than before.

The water is calmer here than where we were by the rocks and I'm glad we were able to yell out our pleasure there. If it had been *here*, we would've had to be a lot quieter.

"You too," I whisper.

I walk through the gate and he follows me, watching until I'm inside. I make sure my mom is still gone as I walk to my room. I peek in her room and she's definitely gone. Hmm. When I reach my room, I look out the window and Raf is standing there. I lift my hand and he lifts his before turning around and walking back into the night.

CHAPTER NINE

I watch for him the next night and he doesn't come.

Or the next night.

I listen for my mom to leave now and she's like clock-work. Around a quarter to eleven, she sneaks out of the house and walks next door. I guess it's a good thing I have this "state of the art" alarm system now because she's certainly not going to be helpful if we have another intruder.

By the third night, I've given up hope that he'll show up again and I jump when I see him standing underneath my window.

I don't know why the sudden change in him and I'm not going to ask. I remind myself of this as I run down the stairs, this time with a blanket that I wear wrapped around my shoulders.

"Couldn't sleep?" I ask.

"Nope."

"How's school?"

"Boring. How's home life?"

"Even more boring than school, if that's possible. But I've gotten a lot of reading in..."

"That doesn't sound too bad."

"I'm hoping my mom will let me out of the house tomorrow night for the game, but so far, she hasn't caved at all. Well, except she gave my phone back today...that's something."

I feel him tense next to me, but he doesn't say anything. We walk the same direction we did the other night and I feel my heart quicken with every step closer to the rocks.

"It's a nice night," I say when he's been quiet for a few minutes.

The waves aren't as loud as the other night. It's actually a calm night, little sound anywhere. Our footsteps are loud against the silence and a shudder of nerves quakes through me.

"You're quiet tonight," I say.

"Or you're chatty."

We reach the rocks and stop, facing each other.

"It's a lot easier when you're not at Longlake," he says, his fingers reaching out to grasp my chin as he lowers his forehead to mine. His touch seems *sweet* and the thought is so weird, especially with his words, and I take a step back. He grabs me with both hands, thinking I'm stumbling.

"Why do you say that?"

"Less to worry about," he says, leaning in to kiss me.

I push him back and he frowns, dropping his hands. "What's wrong?"

"I'm just ready for you to explain yourself." I pull the blanket tighter around my arms, trying to armor myself against whatever he tries to evade next.

He sighs and gives his hair a hard tug. "You can never

just leave things alone, can you?" He sighs again and this time, it sounds angry.

That didn't take long.

"Here we go. You can never just admit what's going on. It's always some game that I have no rules for. You won't even explain what the game *is*..."

He backs up, holding both hands high in front of him. "This was a mistake. I should've known. Nothing can ever be simple with you."

"No, I guess not. I guess I'm not just someone you can stick your dick in and not try to have a normal conversation with once in a while. I've already been abused in that area, thank you. Been there, done that, don't want to do it ever again."

His eyes widen in horror. "Don't you dare compare me to what you had with that prick. This isn't even close to you and Luke and you know it."

"No, I know nothing, Raf. Nothing. Because you give me *nothing*." I don't want to keep talking, but I can't stop myself. "It's been days. I can't just forget everything as quickly as you can."

He takes off walking and I follow him. I don't want to be with him, but I want to be alone on the beach even less. I struggle with the blanket as I lose my grip on it and stumble to keep up with him. When we reach my house, he keeps walking and I turn into my gate, not bothering to say another word.

I should've known whatever we were doing was a disaster waiting to happen. I sneak into the house, not watching where I'm going and run right into a solid chest. I scream and a hand is clasped over my mouth.

"Is that any way to greet your daddy?"

A cold fury clamps around my heart like a vise and I push him away with everything in me.

"How did you get in here?"

"You didn't lock the door on the way out to your little rendezvous with lover boy. He's a good-looking kid. Does he have any interest in the industry, you think?" He laughs like that's the funniest joke he's ever told and I think about how I've never gotten the typical "dad jokes" because they're nothing my dad would ever tell. My father is too perverted to waste time on normal silliness.

I turn away from him and fumble around for my phone under the blanket still draped across my shoulders. I text my mom, at least I hope it's her.

911

And then my phone clatters across the floor as he jerks me around to face him.

"How serious is this side piece with your mother?"

"What are you talking about?"

"Don't play stupid. I know she's seeing someone."

"You probably know better than I do how serious it is."

"I want to hear it from your mouth."

"She seems happy. Happier than you ever made her," I add.

The slap across the face stings, but I'm grateful it wasn't a fist. I drop the blanket, needing the freedom to move quickly if this escalates. I reach down and grab my phone, running across the living room and dialing the police. They answer and the phone is shoved out of my hands and crushed under his boot.

"Why do you insist on disappointing me at every turn, Jocelyn? You make it so hard to be proud of you."

I lift my head up, not bothering to hide my disgust for him. "I could say the same thing about you."

He laughs and his face turns into something hideous when he's this cruel. I hold my hand out for him to sit down, hoping that my mom will get my text and do something to help because I'm not sure I can outrun him. He's going full-throttle tonight, which usually means I'll have a broken bone by the end of the night when he's in this kind of mood.

Or my mom would.

But she's not here, so it's not looking good for me.

"Your videos made me a fortune. Thank you for that. I could've split it with you if you'd let them stay up longer." He laughs again, the sound making my goose bumps stand on end.

I don't say anything, just stare at him, trying to figure out what he wants. He leans forward, his elbows on his knees.

"So you're basically raising yourself here. I could sue for custody on the grounds that you're a minor living alone. I think I'll do that when I get back to Vegas."

My eyes flicker to his and I flinch at the hatred I see there. The scary thing is he could win if he ever tried to fight for me, because he always manages to get his way. He has clout in places he shouldn't, which is why it took my mom a lifetime to get away from him. I doubt custody of me is what he wants. I'm old enough now to put a major crimp in his lifestyle and have been ever since I learned to fight back. But he's evil enough to try if it means making my mom and me miserable.

"I thought you were doing the decent thing for once in your life," I say softly, my lips trembling against my will.

He clasps his hands behind his head and nods. "I allowed you to think that. But you must know that this has gone on long enough."

"Why? Why can't you let us go?"

There's a slight noise behind him, but I don't dare pay attention to it. I shuffle on my feet, trying to make noise and nearly pass out with relief when I see Stefen and three other large men enter the room, guns drawn. My dad lifts his hands and smirks.

"Well, hello, gentlemen. I wondered how long it would take you to get here." He taps his watch and shakes his head. "Sub-par." He stands up and turns to me, his expression a storm ready to break. "Tell your mother I'll be in touch. You shouldn't be left alone here while your stalker is on the loose."

I'm shaking, but when he walks out the door, I collapse on the couch, breathing hard. "Are you going after him?" I ask Stefen.

"There's not much we can do. He left willingly."

"We have a restraining order against him."

"He was able to get a judge to lift that," my mom says behind me.

I turn around, hair flying. I didn't know she was here for any of that. "Why wouldn't you tell me something like that?"

"I didn't want you to worry. I should've told you." She hurries to sit next to me and puts her arms around me. "I'm sorry I wasn't here."

"Yeah, I know you've been leaving," I say under my breath.

The guys go out to make sure my dad is gone.

"How did he get in?" My mom frowns at me. "The alarm system isn't working right. We need to make sure—"

"I went for a walk," I interrupt.

"Jocelyn," she hisses, but low enough that no one else hears. "Why would you do that so late at night when you know how dangerous it is?"

I don't tell her about Raf being with me. I don't want to get either one of us in trouble. "If you'd told me about the restraining order, I wouldn't have."

I fold my hands over my chest. It's been a long night and I'm sick of trying to survive without knowing all the information.

Not even my mother will tell me the truth.

I'm over all the secrets.

Stefen checks the house and the alarm and says he and his men will stay and watch the house throughout the night.

"What about Raf?" I ask Stefen.

"He went to stay with Henry tonight. Left a few hours ago."

I shake my head. "I saw him on the beach right before this happened."

I feel my mom's eyes on me as she waits for me to say more, but I don't. Stefen says something to his men.

"I'll be back. I need to make sure he's okay."

I clutch my mom's hand and wait.

Just knowing my dad is in town makes everything dirty. I rub my arms and feel like I need a shower, something to wash off his words, the way he makes me feel like I'm nothing.

My mom falls asleep while we wait to hear back from Stefen, but the sun rises and he still hasn't come back. And I haven't heard from Raf at all.

I have a horrifying feeling that my dad is to blame for all of this.

CHAPTER TEN

My mom's phone wakes both of us up around nine. She sits straight up after she answers it, her hand clutching her throat.

"Is he okay? Please tell me he's okay," she whispers.

I move closer to her, already tense. "Who is it?"

Her eyes well with tears. "You didn't take him to the hospital? Shouldn't he get checked out?"

I start pacing, my thoughts running wild.

"Okay, I'll get some food for you guys and we'll be over shortly." She hangs up and looks at me. "Do you want to run with me to get takeout?"

"Is it Raf? He's hurt?"

"Yes."

"How bad is it?"

"It sounds like he was beaten pretty badly, but no broken bones and he's conscious."

"Why wasn't he taken to the hospital?"

"Stefen had a friend take a look at him."

"It was Dad, wasn't it?" I don't wait for her to answer, her face saying it all. "Why isn't he arrested right now?

Stefen just let him go after he beat up his son? Why isn't he making him pay?"

"We all want to make him pay. It's just going to take time." Her voice is calmer than I've ever heard it and I stare at her, trying to understand what she's thinking.

I'm so shaken up I can't think straight and my mom seems to be in her element, hurriedly sliding into her boots and throwing a sweater on. She grabs the keys and her purse, chucking her phone into a pocket.

"If you're going with me, let's go. I don't want to waste any time getting over there."

"You know what, I'll meet you over there, okay? I'd like to brush my teeth first."

"I don't want you walking over there alone. Either come with me now or wait for me to get back before you go over there."

"I'll wait," I promise.

"Okay, I'll be back in twenty minutes or so."

The house is creepy now that my dad has been inside it. I'm jumpy, thinking he's going to pop out at any moment. By the time I close my bathroom door and lock it, I'm shaking. I stare in the mirror and try to talk sense into myself. Living with him, I learned a long time ago that I couldn't let fear rule me. Where is that boldness now?

I take a deep breath and shower quickly, not wasting time enjoying the hot water, just going through the motions. I brush my teeth until they bleed and brush my tongue until I gag.

Slow down, hurry up, slow down, hurry up. My thoughts are at war with themselves and I throw on my leggings and a long fitted shirt, searching around the room for something cozy to wear over it if I get cold.

There, on the bed, sits a red lily.

I scream and then cover my mouth, looking wildly around. Nothing else is out of place and I run down the stairs and out to the car, making sure my mom isn't out there anywhere. Her car is gone and I breathe easier, hoping she got out of here with no trouble. I run down the back gate and through Raf's and pound on the back door, breathing hard.

Stefen opens the door and holds me up as I fall inside.

"What's going on—where's your mom?"

"There was another flower on my bed. She went to get food, I think. The car is gone. She told me to stay there, but once I saw the flower, I had to get out of there."

"Slow down. Let me call and make sure she's okay."

I nod and try to catch my breath. I bend down and when I lean back up, I notice Raf lying on the couch. His face is a rainbow of colors, his eye swollen shut and one side of his lips puffier than the other.

I whimper and rush to his side, wanting to touch him but not knowing where I won't hurt him.

"It's not as bad as it looks," he says softly.

"It looks really, really bad." A tear drops down my cheek and Raf's eyes track it.

He reaches out and takes my hand. "Come here. Sit by me." He sits up and clutches his ribs and I try to stop him. "It's fine. I swear it."

We sit facing each other and I haven't let go of his hand.

"You're shaking."

I hear Stefen coming and Raf lets go of my hand.

"I'm okay," he says. "Are you?"

"I just got shaken up. I've been worried about you. And you know, these stupid flowers keep showing up. It could've been put there last night, I guess. Mom and I slept downstairs waiting to hear from you. Maybe my dad left it and I just didn't notice it until today. I don't know." I rub my forehead, trying to smooth away the headache that's building.

"We'll check out the house again today. I didn't notice it last night and I'll ask the guys if they did. We checked, but it's possible we missed it. Did you leave it there?"

"Yes. On my bed."

Raf's eyes flash and he stands up, walking slowly toward his dad. "Find the bastard," he says through gritted teeth.

"You know I will," Stefen says under his breath. He points at Raf. "Get back on that couch. You agreed to rest if I wouldn't take you in. Don't make me regret it."

Raf scowls, but he lies back down.

My mom comes in a few minutes later, and once the door is shut behind her, she rushes to me, hugging me until I can't breathe.

"I shouldn't have left you for a second."

"We don't even know if it happened today."

"Your dad is capable of awful things, but I don't know why he'd be part of this with the flowers. He knows how—" She leaves it hanging and we stare at each other, remembering how crazy it got with Luke.

I'm not sure I believe my father is capable of anything good at this point, but I don't argue with her. And the thought of Luke being inside my house...if it's him, he's getting cocky, which doesn't bode well for me.

I focus on Raf, picking up his ice pack and handing it to him. "You should use this."

I don't know how he can smirk without wincing, the way his face is so bruised, but he manages.

"I should've gotten beat up a long time ago if it meant you'd take care of me," he says low enough that only I can hear.

I flush and I feel my mom's eyes on both of us, so I act

annoyed and walk to the kitchen. She follows me in there and I ask her where the glasses are to distract myself.

"Jos..." She groans. "I just can't seem to get used to calling you Gabriela."

"It seems like they know so much anyway. Why hide my name anymore?"

"What do you want me to call you?"

"I prefer Gabriela or Gabi. I've done my best to shed Jocelyn since we moved here."

She nods. "Okay, I can try to do better. Honey, what's going on with you and Raf? There are times I swear, you guys seem—"

I wait for her to finish and she looks expectantly at me. "Oh, I wanted to see where you were going with that." I try to laugh, but it doesn't sound real. I fill the glass with water and take a long drink. "Nothing is going on between us. We hate each other...most of the time."

"It doesn't look like hate to me."

"Well, trust me, that's all we're capable of."

I hear commotion in the other room and my mom and I exchange a quick look of terror before running into the other room. Raf is slower to get there.

Stefen stands in the entryway trying to contain a livid Heidi. He has her by the arm as she tries to peel his fingers off of her. She's crying and angry.

"Dad?" Raf takes a step forward and Heidi turns on the waterworks more when she sees him.

"Tell him to let me go!" she wails.

"I caught her lurking around Gabriela's car and the house," Stefen says through gritted teeth.

Heidi jerks away and shakes her head wildly. I can't tell if she's on something or just losing it. Stefen shifts her bag off of her arm and it falls to the ground. One of Stefen's men comes in behind them and hovers over her.

The hatred in her eyes toward me is staggering and I take a step back.

"What is your problem with me?" I ask.

Her lips curl and she stares at Raf, desperate again. "I won't let you ruin him."

Raf moves toward her and takes her hand. It's like a deep cut in my side and I nearly bend over with the hurt.

"Let her go, Dad. She's fine." He leans into her ear and whispers something and she brightens, wiping the tears from her face. She nods and he backs away.

"Stay off our property," Stefen says. "You and Raf might be friends, but there's no good that can come out of you trespassing around here like you own the place. Next time you want to see my son, arrange it over the phone. And stay away from Gabriela."

"Yes, sir." She gives Stefen a meek look and when her eyes flash to mine, she's got a smug smile.

I wish I could say I feel relief as she leaves, but I don't. Her little moment with Raf stings. Nothing makes sense.

I try to call Laura. It's less about wanting a drink and more about the downward spiral I'm sinking into. She doesn't answer. Again.

I'm beginning to question everyone.

CHAPTER ELEVEN

Stefen and his team are gone for hours. A few guards stay behind, but they're all outside. Once again, I'm looking for a place to hide in Raf's house.

"Should we go to the police ourselves?" I ask my mom several times while I'm pacing back and forth. "I just don't trust these people—"

"My dad works closely with the station," Raf interrupts. "You need to stay here. He'll let you know if you should go."

I want to bite his head off, my anger still boiling over how he acted with Heidi.

My mom puts her hand on mine, her eyes warning me to keep the peace.

"I didn't know he worked with the police. If you'd told me that from the beginning, it would've helped." I roll my eyes.

"You knew he was an investigator."

"If you only knew how many sleazy 'investigators' I've met," I say, my hands on my hip. "And the fact that he bought Heidi's story doesn't put me at ease at all. If he bought that, he doesn't know what the hell he's doing."

He shrugs and smirks at me over his shoulder. I want to cram his lips down his throat. "My dad is smarter than he looks," he says.

"Right. Well, meanwhile, people seem to still have full access to our houses, despite your *amazing* alarm system. Mom, we need to get out of here." I lean in front of her, getting in her face.

"What made you choose Longlake?" Raf leans back on the couch, stretching out his legs and getting comfortable again.

"It's what Hugh agreed to when we were divorced. He agreed to let us start over, get away from Luke, and he approved of Longlake before she even applied." Mom fists the material of her shirt and then smooths it out, over and over. "What are we missing?"

I turn to Raf and his bruises look so painful, I wince. The guilt that my father did that to him and he's still trying to help us figure all of this out is overwhelming. I feel slightly bad for all the hateful thoughts I've had about him.

"Did your dad know Luke before he came to work for him?"

"No, he couldn't have," Mom says. She turns to me. "Right?"

"If he did, they both lied about it."

All three of us are quiet then, the implications of this too troubling to voice out loud.

I call Ashton and it goes straight to voicemail. I feel terrible about missing his game, but it's too dangerous right now. And after Raf got hurt so badly, the thought of putting

Ashton at risk is too much to take. I can't put him or Luci in any danger.

I leave a message.

"Ashton, I'm so sorry. I wanted to come to your game tonight so bad. There are crazy things going on with my family. We had a break-in. I thought I might be able to talk my mom into letting me go this one night, but she's watching me like a hawk more than ever. I know you're going to do great and wish I could see you. Call me later and let me know how it went."

It's late before Stefen gets home. I hear him come in and am upstairs in the guest bedroom. I'm too tired to go downstairs to hear what he's saying and when I check my phone, I'm disappointed that Ashton never called. I hope they won.

The next morning, Stefen and my mom are talking outside on the deck when I come downstairs. Raf isn't around and I wander around the kitchen, unsure if I should make a piece of toast or if that's too presumptuous since this isn't my house. There's coffee and I pour half a cup, not willing to be so polite that I don't get my coffee.

I check my phone again and there's a text from Ashton.

Ashton: Hey, I'm really sorry—just saw this a little bit ago. Where are you? I'm at your house.

I'm at Raf's.

I see dots and then they disappear. A few minutes later, the doorbell rings and I freeze. It rings again as my phone vibrates.

Ashton: I'm at the door. :) You letting me in or what?

I hurry to the door just as Raf is walking down the stairs. He's shaking his head.

"Don't answer that."

"It's Ashton."

He frowns. "What's he doing here?"

I turn and open the door. Ashton walks in and gives me a huge hug. "Are you okay? What happened?"

Raf clears his throat and when we both turn to him, he's radiating all his angry heat our way. Ashton frowns when he sees Raf's face.

"What happened to you?"

"Nothing," Raf says, folding his arms across his chest.

"Uh, yeah, looks like it," Ashton snorts, turning to me for answers.

"How did the game go?" I decide to forego the drama since I don't even know where to begin to explain any of it.

"We won." He grins and I wrap my arm around his waist, giving him another side hug.

"That's great. Congratulations."

"Thanks. The bigger news of the night had nothing to do with the game, though...we had another overdose." He looks past me to Raf.

"Who? What happened?" Raf asks.

"Sheree Monson—freshman. She collapsed by concessions. As far as I know she's still alive."

"That's awful. Did they arrest anyone?"

"No, but I bet they'll get more intense at school over the drugs. Longlake is supposed to be the straight and narrow. Can't have word getting out that we're turning into a bunch of druggies." Ashton lifts a shoulder.

"You probably have no idea since you were playing, but

has anyone said anything about Heidi being there or involved in this?"

He shakes his head. "I haven't heard anything about her, no."

"Well, thanks for stopping by," Raf says.

My eyes narrow on his and he smirks, daring me to argue with him.

"Uh, sure. You okay, Gabi?" Ashton looks down at me. "There was a break-in?"

"The police are still trying to figure it all out. That's why I'm here instead of my house."

He nods, glancing over my shoulder at Raf. "Well, let me know if I can do anything. You're welcome to come to my house too, you know."

A choked sound comes from Raf behind me and I roll my eyes. "Thank you. I'll call you later."

"See ya," Raf says. He comes to stand by me and opens the door, opening it wide.

"See ya, asshole," Ashton says.

I giggle and he smiles at me before turning and walking out.

"It's true, you know," I tell Raf once the door is shut.

"Never tried to pretend otherwise," he says.

"How about you go hang out with Heidi and leave me alone about Ashton?"

"How about you quit trying to use Ashton as bait? He doesn't deserve that. He's a good guy."

"A much better guy than you." I roll my eyes again.

He has the audacity to look wounded.

I shake my head and go upstairs. It's too early to deal with his stupidity.

I do homework and watch Netflix, ignoring my hunger pains. When I come downstairs, there's a note from my mom saying she'll be back later. Two guards are stationed outside and one is inside.

Raf is chatting with him when I go into the living room and they stop talking when they see me.

"Where did my mom go?" I ask them.

"No idea," Raf says.

"I'm Carl. I'll be watching things here until they get back." He's a big guy, his shoulders wider than my thighs.

"Did they say when they'd be back?"

He shakes his head.

I go upstairs and text my mom.

Where are you?

It's a few hours before she responds and when she does, it's cryptic.

Mom: It looks like I won't be back until tomorrow night. There are extra guards surrounding the house for your protection. I'm sorry I wasn't able to tell you before I left, sweetie. I love you. Rest and I'll explain more when I get back.

You seriously left me here alone with Raf and random guards?

She doesn't say anything and I come up with a thousand different ways to chew her out when she gets back.

CHAPTER TWELVE

I sneak down to the kitchen a few hours later. I don't care how rude it seems, I'm scrounging around in this kitchen until I find something to eat. I should've been checking on Raf throughout the day, making sure he was feeling okay, but I'm so mad at him, I haven't bothered.

He's chowing down on a pizza when I come in the kitchen. He looks slightly guilty when he sees me and then his shoulders straighten like they always do when he's daring me to confront him.

"Nice of you to let me know there was food."

"I figured if you were hungry, you'd come down."

"Asshole," I mutter under my breath.

"That you love to fuck," he says under his.

My eyes flash to his and he's staring at me, his eyes roaming up my body slowly, pausing on my legs and then my breasts before eventually working up to my lips and eyes. I know I'm red by the time he gets to my face, and I wish I could turn around and slam the door in his face, but my stomach is growling too much to do that.

I pick up a slice of pizza and eat all of it before sitting down and picking up another slice.

"My mom says she'll be back tomorrow night. Any idea where they went?"

"No idea. I don't have a good feeling about it though."

"Why? What are you thinking?"

"I'm wondering if they went to Vegas or something...to see if they could find Luke. Or to follow your dad maybe."

"Why wouldn't Stefen keep my mom out of it? Does he care about her at all?" My voice hikes up at the end and I put my head in my hands.

"Relax. He's looking out for her. We may not like it, but I think they care about each other."

"You better be right." I drop my hands and take a few bites of pizza. "Why didn't they tell us what they were doing? My mom likes to keep me in the dark, but it's not like her to leave at a time like this. I can't believe she'd leave the state without letting me know...or taking me with her. With my dad being in town? It's just so weird."

"It was a theory. They could be in a hotel across town for all I know. Maybe they want to be loud when they fuck." He shrugs.

I throw my crust at him, knocking him in the forehead. He lifts both eyebrows.

"Really. We're throwing things at each other now?"

"Don't talk about our parents fucking."

"Ah, right. How can I forget? You like your daily dose of denial." He laughs when I lift another slice of pizza, ready to smash it in his face. Instead, he takes it out of my hand and takes a big bite, talking with his mouth full. "Listen, my dad isn't exactly keeping me in the loop right now either. I tried to get Carl to spill, but he's not saying a word."

I take a few more bites of pizza droppings left on my

plate and feel better, even with all the anxiety coursing through my veins. At least I'm full.

"Want to watch a movie or something?" Raf asks.

"I guess that would be okay."

"What...you gotta check with your mother?" He lifts his shoulders and I glare at him while he laughs.

I open my mouth and he beats me to it.

"I know, I know. I'm an asshole. So do you want to or not?"

"Ugh. You're so annoying."

"Yeah, yeah."

I help him pick up. He puts the plates in the dishwasher while I wipe down the table. I assume we'll go back to the living room to watch a movie, but he motions for me to follow him down to the basement.

"I had no idea this was down here. We don't have many basements in Vegas."

It's a huge room and there's a massive screen and plush sectional with blankets and pillows everywhere.

"This is where my dad and I hang out the most...or we used to."

"What changed?"

"Our parents started dating, for one."

I groan.

"And he works a lot," he pauses. "Things got a little weird between the two of us for a while too, when he was so adamantly against my music. I guess we've been better again, but it's still not normal."

"That sucks, especially if you're usually close. Are you?"

"Yeah. It's been hard."

"I don't understand why he wouldn't just want you to be happy."

"Even my dad has certain standards. Every parent at Longlake has the same disease: perfect child syndrome-itis."

"Except for being a class A jerk, it seems like you're doing everything else right as far as what your dad sees."

He gives me a sideways glance and turns the TV on. "It kills you to compliment me, doesn't it?"

"That wasn't a compliment. Clearly, your dad is in the dark about who you really are."

He shifts so our shoulders are touching and I feel the heat through our clothes. I move away just enough that it's not obvious, but I can feel him looking at me. I stare at the screen, trying to focus on anything but the way my body craves his.

"What do you want to watch?" His voice is low and raspy and it stirs something in me that I can't ignore.

"You know what? I think I might be too tired to start a movie now."

He's quiet and then I feel his fingers on my chin as he turns me to face him.

"Gabi? You're not afraid to watch a movie with me, are you?"

I crinkle my forehead, frowning as hard as I physically can with his hand on my face. "What? No," I scoff.

He smiles and I lose all capability of reasoning. My eyes are drawn to his lips and when they edge closer to me, my breath catches in my throat.

"What about Heidi?" I whisper.

"Forget her," he whispers back.

He kisses me softly, little nips along my lower lip and then his tongue flicks its way inside. I whimper into his mouth and his hand dives into my hair, pulling me closer.

I lose myself in his kiss for a long time, but when he

pulls me over so I'm straddling him and I rock against his hardness, my head falls back and he kisses down my neck.

"I don't think I'll ever stop wanting you," he whispers against my skin.

"This is the last time. It has to be," I whisper. "We can't keep doing this and then hating each other more afterward."

He doesn't say anything and I lean back to look at him. His fingers trace circles over my nipples and then he pulls my shirt off, his eyes worshipping me. He undoes my bra and when it falls off, he groans and arches into me. He lifts me up and I put my feet on the ground, standing in front of him as he follows me. He slides my leggings down and pulls his shirt off with one hand as he gets on his knees and motions for me to lie back on the couch. I sit down and he situates me until my panties are in his face.

"We don't need these," he says, sliding them off and making me shiver when his warm breath hits my sensitive skin.

When he gives my slit a long lick, I groan and so does he. And the fury he unleashes on me in the next breath is on another level. I try to be quiet in case the guards are listening, but it's like he knows and pulls out all of his tricks to make me explode. I put one of the pillows over my mouth when he starts sucking me hard and he pulls the pillow off.

"Let me hear you. I want to hear everything," he says, wiping his mouth and going back in.

I lose it in the next breath, when he goes faster and faster, eating me until I can't think straight. I seize and come apart against his tongue and he rides it out with me until I am only slightly clenching around him still. Cool air hits my skin as he lifts up and his cock is inside me within the next breath.

"Condom?" I gasp.

He pulls out and hurriedly slides one on. "Sorry. I'm so —I lost my mind for a second."

He secures it and tugs me forward, propping my legs on his shoulders. When he thrusts into me, my eyes roll back. He tweaks my nipples and I feel like I could come again that fast. He starts an unrelenting tempo that feels as desperate and out of control as I feel and I open my eyes and watch him. His expression is fierce and determined and he stares at me with such lust I shudder against him.

"What is this?" I whimper.

"Admit you want me," he says, his hand reaching between us to rub me in tiny circles.

"No," I moan, my eyes fluttering shut against their will.

He pulls his hand away and my eyes fly open again. He slows down drastically, pulling way out and slowly driving back in, and I try to speed him up, to get back to that explosive way we were just seconds ago.

"Admit it." He lowers his mouth to my breast and takes my nipple between his teeth and then flicks it with his tongue. He's going deeper and harder but still not as fast as I want.

I lean up until my chest is against his and I push him back until he's on his back as I straddle him. I set the pace then and he lets me for a few seconds, trying to control me with his hands on my hips, but when I start circling over him faster and faster, his mouth parts and I know he's losing control fast.

"Gabi." His voice is anguished when I clench around him and he jerks inside me as we come together.

He pulls me against his chest and we catch our breath together. I didn't admit anything out loud, but I think our bodies said everything for us.

CHAPTER THIRTEEN

Once I've had a few seconds to come down from my high, I'm embarrassed. Why do I keep letting this happen?

I pull away and stand up, grabbing my clothes from the floor.

"Gabi—"

"I'm just gonna go to bed," I say quietly.

"Don't, please—stay."

I hold up my hand and he stops, his face unreadable when I risk looking at him. Suddenly, all I can think about is how he defended Heidi. I feel like the fool all over again.

I quickly put my clothes on and am to the door when he says just loud enough for me to hear: "I didn't take you for a coward."

Humiliation stings my eyelids and I pause but keep walking and don't turn back. Once the door is shut to the bedroom, I slide to the floor and cry. Why do I keep putting myself through this shame, this guilt, this humiliation?

I'm a broken record. Raf is the last person I should want.

But I do. I want him with everything in me.

It's a while before I pick myself off of the floor and get my shower. I'm in bed when I hear Raf go into his room and close the door.

It takes an eternity to go to sleep.

When I wake up the next morning, I'm already exhausted, imagining another day of trying to ignore Raf in this house. I can't wait for my mom to get back and for us to go home. Everything is so unsettled. It'll feel weird being home too, but anything will be better than this.

I don't have much of an appetite, so it's easier to hide. I eventually make my way downstairs when I get too thirsty to ignore it. I listen for noise downstairs and sometimes hear Raf with the guards, but when all is quiet for a few hours, I sneak down to the kitchen. I gather a few snacks and drinks and get the ice last.

My phone pings with several texts in a row and I nearly drop my snacks in my hurry to see who it is. I'm so mad at my mom I can't think straight.

I haven't heard from her since yesterday.

Luci: I'm scared, Gabi. There's a new video of you.

What? Where? When did you see it?

Luci: Someone I didn't know sent me a hard copy.

Who? How? I don't understand. I need to see it.

Luci: My parents aren't letting me leave the house. Can you come get it? I don't want them to find it. With all the questions the cops are

asking about Jen, they're threatening to make me change schools.

Hide it. I'll come as soon as I can.

I put the snacks away, go back upstairs, and change into my jeans. I pause outside Raf's door, but I'm too keyed up about the video. I can't stand the tension I know will be there between us in the light of day. He's like a bad hangover, every day-after worse than the last time I partook.

I wait until I hear him leave his room, listening when it sounds like he stops outside my room and then moves down the stairs. He goes out the door and I move to the window to see what he does next. He starts running when he reaches the back gate and I decide to make my move while I have the chance.

There's a guard outside the door and I point toward my house.

"I just need to get something really quick. I'll be back in a minute."

He nods but then proceeds to follow me. I sigh, wondering how I'm gonna get to Luci's without him on my tail. And then wonder what would be the problem with that. I'm free to leave.

"I need to run out for a while," I tell him.

"Okay, give me a minute. I'll follow."

I nod and get in my car, watching as he walks next door and disappears to his car. I grin, pleased that he didn't get in the car with me. It hits me that I'm wasting time. I start the car and don't wait for him, pulling out of the driveway and speeding to Luci's. From the rearview mirror, I see him pull out, but I'm too far ahead of him now and lose him easily. My phone starts going off when I'm a few blocks from Luci's and I ignore it. I don't have to look to know it's probably Raf calling to chew me out for leaving.

It feels so good to get out of the house that I don't even feel bad for disappearing on them. I'm not doing anything crazy, I just want to see Luci, maybe Ashton if I get a chance...and not have Raf hanging over our interactions like a jealous old man. Okay, maybe it's a little crazy, but I'm going to be careful.

I pull up to Luci's house and text her, letting her know I'm here. I don't bother waiting to hear back before I get out of the car. She knew I would hustle over here.

I rarely come to Luci's house. It's a little off the beaten path. A pretty house in a different neighborhood than most of the kids from school, she lives in a smaller place with ivy growing along the front of the house. She prefers to come to my house, so I've never pushed, but if my mom keeps forcing us to stay with Raf, I'm going to spend a lot more time here.

Once I'm out of the car, I put my phone in my pocket and feel the hair on the back of my neck stand up. I look around to see if anyone is watching me and all is quiet. *Too quiet.* I pick up my pace and am a few feet from the door before I slow down again. A cloth goes over my face and my arms flail, everything fading to black.

I wake up in a fog, sitting up slowly and looking around. I'm in a bed and I almost expect to be tied down somehow, but I'm completely free. The room is all white and pretty. No windows, but a lamp is on next to the bed. I think I hear the beach and listen for anything else that might give me a clue of where I am. There's a small bathroom on the left with the door open, the tiles of a shower barely showing from here. I stand up and pause, holding my head. I'm dizzy for a few seconds and once I have my bearings, I go to the bedroom door and turn the knob. Locked.

I slam my fist against the door.

"Let me out of here," I yell.

Probably not the smartest move, but it seems like I'll have to see my captor eventually. Why not speed up the process?

My next thought, ironically, is school. I've missed too much since starting Longlake. I have to get out of here and make sure nothing else gets between me and graduating.

Why that's on my mind now, I don't know.

When no one comes and I've searched the entire room for my phone (it's not here) or something to tell me ANYTHING about this place or who has me (there's nothing), I fall back on the bed and stare at the ceiling.

Tears drip back into my hair.

And then more anger.

Pacing.

Hours of my stomach turned inside out, gnawing with hunger.

And still, no one comes.

I imagine what Raf must be thinking now. He's going to be so mad at me. My mom will finally feel bad for leaving me at the house, as she should. And in the next thought, I'm internally beating myself up for leaving the house and taking off before the guard could follow me. *How could I be so stupid?*

Once again, I've managed to screw everything up. Between Luke and my father, there's no telling what kind of mess I've gotten myself in now.

But which is it? Luke or my father?

CHAPTER FOURTEEN

I fall asleep at some point, my last thought that I could never fall asleep with how hungry I am, how afraid, but I wake with a start. I hear voices in the distance but can't make out what they're saying. It's too hard to tell if they're familiar voices, but I get up and go to the door, straining to listen.

How long did I sleep?

I go to the bathroom and pace, wishing there was a window to distract myself. A way to tell the time. Anything to feel some sense of where I am.

The door opens sometime later, after I'm exhausted with more pacing, and I stand up, taking a step backward when I see a Donald Trump mask over a skinny body. I swallow hard, feeling hysteria rising in my chest, and try to figure out if I recognize the body underneath the baggy clothes. They're slight. No matter how hard they're trying to disguise with all the clothes, they're not much taller than me.

A tray is placed on the table and the person leaves without a word.

"Wait!" I rush toward the door and pound until my fingers burn. "Come back. What do you want from me?" I yell and then the rest of what comes out feels like jumbled nonsense of me venting as they probably sit outside and laugh. I sag against the door when I start crying, not wanting them to hear my desperation.

Desperation breeds...nothing good. Or something like that. I know there's a quote about what exactly desperation breeds, but it's not fully formulating in my mind right now.

The smell of the food wafts across the room and I get up, taking the tray to the bed. I sniff it. Would I be able to tell if it were laced with anything? And what do I care anyway? It's either die of starvation or die of drug-laced food.

It's only day one...or two, depending on how long you slept. Day one if I'm going by how exhausted I still feel. You're not dying of anything yet, I ramble to myself.

Cheeseburger and fries. Looks like a Shake Shack burger or something from a diner, and I wrinkle my nose as I try to decide if I'm too picky to eat the slab of unmelted American cheese. I'm more of a feta on my burger kind of girl.

I want to slap myself for my snotty thoughts.

I take a deep breath and go in for a bite, quickly inhaling the burger. It's divine, unmelted American cheese and all.

I take a long swig of the drink and grimace—diet soda, yuck—but a pleasant feeling washes down my gut. Because with this drink, I know something.

It's a girl keeping me here or at least picking out the food. A guy would never bring a diet drink.

I finish eating and once that's settled, I exercise, hoping I'll be ready when I see someone again. What's with the

Donald Trump face? I shiver but try to focus on the adrenaline pumping through my body.

I hear voices outside the door again, this time closer, and my heart pounds out of my chest. I still can't make out what they're saying and my anger skyrockets. I can't believe they're holding me here like this.

I pound on the door again. "Are you gonna show yourself? Too much of a wuss to show your face?"

The voices stop and I lift my hand to pound again when it opens. I fall forward and muscled arms hold onto either side of my arms, pushing me back.

"Luke," I whisper. My stomach gnarls into a painful swirl of hatred and nausea and I try to pry myself out of his grip.

"Hey, baby. I have you right where I want you." He grins and black spots dance across my vision. I fight to not pass out, my eyes widening as I struggle to hang on.

"What do you want with me?" I ask, panting hard. He lets me go abruptly and I fall to the ground. I scramble backward until I hit the wall and he laughs.

"I'm glad to see you recognize the danger of the situation you're in. Finally." He presses his hands together. "You're not in charge of this, Jocelyn. How does that feel?"

"I don't go by Jocelyn anymore," I snap. I remember now how much I started hating the way my name sounded across his lips. When I decided I was done with him and he turned into my tormentor. It all floods back and I start shaking. I've tried so hard to forget.

It was as if my avoiding him turned him on more. I saw a different side of him when I told him no. All of a sudden, the lilies were everywhere I turned, school, the coffee shop, my bedroom. And he was always there, lurking and grinning what I now saw as his sick smile. He tried to force himself on me one of those late nights, as I was rushing to my car from the bookstore. It turned everything between us even uglier. I knew I couldn't handle it on my own anymore, but I was too afraid to tell my parents.

"You'll always be Jocelyn to me." His voice brings me back to the present and he shrugs nonchalantly, like he knows I've gotten lost in the past. He reaches his hand out, expecting me to latch onto it, and I take it, standing up slowly in front of him. "Here's how we'll play this," he says, motioning for me to sit down on the bed.

I do. The last thing I want is to be anywhere near a bed with him, but I need to see what he wants before I decide how I will fight.

"Your father owes me money." He runs his fingers along my jawline and then grips it tightly, yanking my head back to look him in the eye. My eyes fill with tears. "And you owe me time. I paid my dues in that cold cell you sent me to— how do you think that made me feel?" His fingers dig into my skin and I gasp. "It hurt. Memories of your tight little body kept me going, so I do have to thank you for that. If you weren't the reason I was there in the first place, this would be such a sweet reunion." He laughs and I close my eyes, tears running down my face. "No tears." I feel his tongue on my cheek and feel my food rising up my throat. "No tears," he says again, his voice harsh this time. "You'll give me what I want and then I'll decide whether it's enough to let you go."

"I thought you were working with Stefen. What was that about?"

He grins and it's unbelievable that I ever thought he was so good looking. How does anyone look at him and see beauty? All I see is rot.

"I have my hand in a few pots," he says. "And you're the

sweet honey in all of them. My little honey pot." His voice slithers over me and he rips the neck of my shirt, baring my chest. Someone enters the room and I try to peer around him to see who it is, but he holds me in place with his hands around my neck.

Out of the corner of my eye, I see video cameras rolling in, large ones similar to those I saw the one time I snuck to my mom's set. I want answers, but I can tell by the way he's glancing around now, that his attention is on whatever scene he's creating. Mirrors are brought in and two cameras on either side of the bed. Two people, both in masks—one Frida Kahlo on a huge burly frame, and the other Bill Clinton on a smaller but muscular frame—work on getting the cameras ready. I don't see Donald anywhere and part of me wishes the girl was here for this. Maybe I could appeal to her feminine sensibilities before I'm raped on camera.

A spotlight turns on and Luke rips the rest of my clothes off, leaving me in my underwear. He makes a sound with his mouth, assessing me and shaking his head like he's so disappointed.

"You used to have much better taste," he says.

He unhooks my bra and I try to dodge his hands and cover myself with the blanket from the bed, but he's too fast. He hauls me up and rips my panties off with one hand, leaving me naked in front of three men.

CHAPTER FIFTEEN

I'm too mad to cry, but my body betrays me and the tears drip down my face anyway. I feel like a rag doll, the way he dresses me in a new lacy bra and panty set and then slides a silk floral dress on me. It's long and demure. Pretty even. I barely register the approval in his eyes when he looks at me, the way he presses himself against me, hard under his pants.

I used to be proud of the way I could make him want me, but when I realized he used drugs to get hard like that, it whittled my pride down to nothing.

He leans back and grins and twirls me around, my dress unfurling around my legs, the breeze sending shivers up my spine. He turns me until I'm dizzy and in the next second brings me to a dead stop. I'm unsteady on my feet, so I don't even see his hand until it's near my face, the slap resounding. I step back and he advances, reaching out and giving my dress a yank so hard that the material splits down the middle, leaving my skin exposed.

His grin widens and he shoves me back on the bed. I scuttle backwards, trying to get away, making him laugh. I look over his shoulder and see the light flashing on the cameras. He's not bothering to hide that he's recording all of this now.

I imagine everyone at school seeing this and my skin heats with the shame. Why did I think I could ever outrun him?

Somewhere between him stripping out of his clothes and ripping off my panties to shreds, I decide to fight. It's a bit delayed, but maybe that works in my favor. I knee him in the balls and when his hand reaches out for my neck to choke me, I duck and bite him so hard, I immediately taste blood. He screeches for help and the cameramen just stand there, momentarily in shock.

When he reaches back and punches my face, I take a breath and let go of his skin, shoving him off of me with adrenaline I didn't know I had.

"You fucking bitch!" He yanks me by the hair and slings me back on the bed, his eyes predatory. "You wanna fight?"

"It's the only way you'll have me," I tell him. And I spit out his blood, watching as it lands on his face and rolls down his chin.

He looks demented and I'm sure I don't look much better. He crawls off of me and signals for the cameras to stop recording.

"Guess we'll have to go with Plan B," he says. His smile sends a slither over my skin. "It was my preference anyway."

I press my hand to my cheek, feeling the puffy skin where he hit me. I'm relieved he stopped for now, but from the look on his face, it only means it will be worse for me later. I don't know how I know that, I just do. He looks too cocky for someone who has been shut down.

I grab the blanket and pull it over me as he stands up and walks over to one of the cameras. I hear a few clicks and then he pauses when he hears something in the house. I don't miss the look that passes between him and the other men, but instead of saying anything else, he rolls one camera out and the others follow. The door shuts behind them and I'm left alone again.

I go to the bathroom and take a long shower, feeling like I've dodged a bullet, but the dread for what will come next, the unknown, is so heavy, I stagger under its weight.

After hours of waiting for him to come back, the fear settling in my bones like a rattly winter cough, I wonder if this was what he intended for me all along. He must be watching somewhere—I know there are cameras still hidden here somewhere—loving how I can't relax, the fear I can't hide, the way I haven't slept or eaten anything they've left. I'm hot with the clothes I was in before he had me change, clinging to my skin, but still I put my head under the covers, anything to not let him get an advantage over me. I don't want him to see me or know anything about me. I've felt that for a long time now.

I avoided telling my parents about Luke for as long as I could, but he got more and more erratic after the night outside the bookstore. What seemed annoying at first—him turning up everywhere I went—became sinister when he wouldn't back off. He followed me home one night when he knew my parents were at a work event and pounded on the door for an hour. I didn't know what to do. I wanted to call the police, but I was too afraid of what my parents would think. As it turned out, I was such a wreck by the time they came home, I had to come clean to my mom about what was going on.

I was shaking and crying, huddled on the floor of my bedroom. She came and sat beside me.

"Luke won't leave me alone," I whispered.

"Is this a guy from school?" She shook her head, puzzled that she couldn't think of which Luke I would mean.

I shook my head and it took a few moments before it registered.

"Luke from work?"

I nodded and the blood rushed from her face.

The first thing she said was, "Your father will kill him." And then, "Just how serious has it been with him?" I knew she was still hoping I hadn't had sex with him.

When she realized how far it had gone, she was so upset, she went straight to my dad. I stood outside their room, wringing my hands, worried and yet relieved to not carry this secret by myself any longer.

My father put Luke in the hospital that night and still managed to get off without so much as a warning because of his friends on the police force. When they searched his room and found the videos of him having sex with an underage girl (me), they arrested him, and for a few blissful months, my home was peaceful.

It all went haywire when the first video of me showed up online. My mom blamed my father. My father blamed Luke. And I didn't know who to blame.

Before Luke, we'd maintained a peaceful front here and there. Seasons of peace that never lasted, but we all played our part. I knew my parents' marriage was a facade, but *After* Luke, there was no pretense.

I was the slut in my father's eyes, and my mom was the slut who'd raised me. It didn't matter that my father had held the strings to my mother's career all along. Suddenly, we were dirt in his eyes. And Luke, well, my father would've probably killed him if he hadn't figured out a way to send him to prison instead.

The violence I'd been accustomed to at home combusted...until a stalker felt easier to manage than getting knocked around by my father and nursing my mother's wounds.

———

I hear voices outside my door and burrow further under the covers. *Please, please, leave me alone.* I'm so tired. The fight from earlier has drained out of me and I don't feel like I have it in me to keep him from doing whatever he wants. I hear a voice that sounds familiar and I sit up in bed, the blanket falling off of me.

"You have to leave her. She's not worth it, Luke."

I'd know that grating tone anywhere. The door opens and the girl in the Donald mask is back, but now I know exactly who it is.

Heidi.

CHAPTER SIXTEEN

She rushes in, gripping the bottom edge of the Donald mask near her neck as she comes straight for me.

"What are you doing here?" I ask. I stop myself right before saying her name, but it's as if I've said it by the way she stops and stares, or at least I think she's looking at me. It's hard to tell with the mask.

Luke comes in behind her, holding a hypodermic needle. I get off of the bed and run to the bathroom and think Heidi is coming after me to stop me, but she manages to block Luke.

"Think about it," she whispers. "Do you really want to go back to prison?"

"Get out of my way," he roars.

"It's one thing to do an anonymous video, Luke, and another to inject her and show your face on camera. Think about this," she yells. And if I had any doubts before that it was Heidi, they're all gone now.

I'm shocked she's trying to reason with him. Even if it's for his sake, I'm grateful she's prolonging the inevitable.

"Get out of my fucking way." I hear a strike and a yelp of pain, and the sound of someone falling into the door.

The bathroom door doesn't lock, so when he opens the door wide, stepping over Heidi's body, I know there's no way out of this one. He holds the needle up and advances toward me in what feels like slow motion. I close my eyes and prepare for the worst.

Instead, there's a loud thud and Luke's body falls against mine. I open my eyes and Toby is standing there holding a gun. He puts an unconscious and bloody Luke in handcuffs and then holds out his hand, helping me to my feet.

The room fills with men and guns. I can't tell if they're cops or what, and Toby isn't saying a word. He puts his arm around me and helps me out the door, leading me to an SUV with tinted windows.

"Are you going to tell me how a high school student just saved me from being drugged and raped on camera?" I ask before climbing into the vehicle.

"We have mutual friends," he says with a smile. "And I'm a bit older than you think."

"I sort of knew but didn't have proof." I smile back.

He opens the door for me and I get in. He walks around and gets behind the wheel just as cop cars pull up to the house and run inside.

"We're not sticking around to talk to them?" I turn and look back as we drive away.

"No. You'll have your chance to talk to them later. I think you've been traumatized enough, don't you?"

I lean my head against the back of the seat and sigh. "Thank you. The last thing I want to do is spend hours at the police station." I turn to look at him. "Is Luci okay? Tell me she isn't part of all this."

"No, she wasn't. Her phone was stolen and she had no idea you were ever at her place."

My shoulders sag, relieved Luci wasn't involved or hurt. "So Laura?"

He cringes. "Yeah. I didn't realize right away that you knew my sister. She nearly destroyed my cover."

"She fell off the face of the earth."

"Sorry about that. She panicked when I let her know you were involved in one of my cases. You can have your sponsor back."

"I think I'm doing okay." And that I'll probably get a new sponsor if I'm ever not okay...it would be awkward to continue with her after everything that's happened. "Why were you at the school for so long?"

"The drugs Heidi and Luke have brought into the school systems around here—not just Longlake, but multiple schools in this area—they had to be stopped. And they will be, thanks to you. I was there to bring Heidi down, but you were able to lead us to Luke, her cousin and boss."

I stare at Toby with wide eyes and he chuckles when he looks at me.

"I've gotta hand it to you," he says. "You put up with that bitch far better than I ever would have."

I turn to stare out the front window, thinking about Heidi and the way she saved me with Luke. "She kept Luke from drugging me."

He clears his throat and lifts his eyebrows when I face him again. "Maybe her conscience was finally catching up with her."

We pull into Raf's driveway. It's filled with cars. "What's going on here?"

"You've been missing for two days. This has been the hub. Half of them are at the house we just left—a few people are anxious to see you. Thought I'd let you see them before you have to start answering the questions."

"Thank you. Again. For everything."

He smiles and we get out. My mom comes flying out of the door and wraps her arms around me. I see Raf and Ashton behind her and then behind them all stands my father.

"What is he doing here?" I ask.

My mom pulls back and shakes her head, tears running down her cheeks. "I couldn't keep him out of this. He's talking crazy, but he deserves to know you're okay."

"What kind of crazy?" I frown.

Ashton steps forward then and hugs me hard and my mom moves away. I feel Raf's presence close by and my face heats from the fire I see in his eyes when I glance at him. Ashton kisses my forehead.

"We were so scared," he says. "Raf and I have been losing our minds."

Raf swallows hard and gives the slightest nod. I hold my hand out to him and he takes it, squeezing almost painfully, and then moves forward until I am in his arms.

I'm quiet, soaking in how good it feels to touch him, to be away from that awful room, free of Luke...

I pull back and look over my shoulder at my dad standing there. His look unsettles me, but I turn back to Raf, ignoring the stress of having my dad in the same room.

"So you knew about Toby?" I ask.

Raf nods. It's not like him to be so quiet, but I feel him assessing the damage to my face and the way I wince when I move too quickly. His hands form into fists as he takes a deep breath.

"I didn't until today," Ashton says. "Didn't know a lot of

things until today. Like the fact that Heidi has been selling drugs at Longlake for over a year now."

"Is it really over?" I ask.

My mom puts her arm around me and drags me away from Raf, her eyes cutting up to his with warning signs. I look back at him nervously and he watches us walk away, his face unreadable.

"Stefen is going to make sure both Luke and Heidi pay for what they've done," she says.

We walk toward the house and my father reaches out to stop me when I get close enough.

"Are you okay, Jocelyn?" he asks.

"I'm fine," I tell him, swallowing the lump in my throat.

He nods. "We'll talk tomorrow, okay?"

All of a sudden, I want to be in my room, away from everyone, but my mom leads me into Raf's house and up the stairs to the guest room.

"How about I run you a hot bath?" she asks.

I nod and sit on the edge of the bed while she goes into the bathroom. I hear the water and close my eyes, imagining the scene in that bedroom...what *could've* happened if I hadn't been saved.

My mom clears her throat and I look up. She stands in the doorway staring at me.

"It's over, Gabi. You're safe now. Luke won't get out of prison this time." Her eyes narrow. "What did he do to you?"

I shake my head. "I was mostly alone, but it was about to get a lot worse."

"He hurt you." She skims my face with her fingers and tilts my face to the side.

"I'm okay," I whisper. "What's really going on with Dad? I don't want him here."

"I don't like it any more than you do, trust me. But he showed up with one of his cop friends, demanding his right to be here. Hopefully now that he's seen you, he will leave." Her jaw clenches and she squares her shoulders. "Are you hungry? Can I get you anything? A hot tea while you're in the bath?"

"That sounds nice. I don't want to be in the tub long, but it does sound good."

She nods, looking happy to have something to do.

I move to the bathroom when she leaves the room, and sink into the water a few minutes later, thankful that this ordeal with Luke is finally over.

CHAPTER SEVENTEEN

I'm in my warmest pajamas and flipping the channels in bed, unable to sleep but not wanting to go downstairs either. After my bath, I had to talk to the police for a few hours and my mind is numb. Raf seems angry or maybe that's just the way he shows concern. He stayed by my side downstairs and glared at anyone who asked me anything.

A soft knock on the door makes me jump and my mom peeks through the door. "Luci is here. Are you up to seeing her?"

I don't really feel like seeing anyone, but I nod. I *would* like to see Luci. She's left messages saying how awful she feels about everything.

She comes in a few minutes later and stands in the doorway, hesitant.

"Come in." I wave her over and she sits on the bed facing me. She frowns as she looks at my bruised face and I try to smile to reassure her I'm fine.

"I just feel so bad," she starts.

"It wasn't your fault. You can't help it that Luke stole your phone."

"I still have no idea how it happened or how he was able to figure out my password—well, it was a dumb password, but lesson learned. I'll be smarter next time." She leans forward. "Are you really okay?"

"I am. It was scary and it felt like I was there much longer than I was, but everything could've been so much worse. I'm lucky that it wasn't and that he's finally going away, hopefully for good. Kidnapping charges can't just go away, can they?"

She shakes her head and I pat the space next to me.

"Wanna watch a movie? I'm so tired but don't think I can sleep."

"Sure." She moves into place and we watch *Legally Blonde*.

She leaves when that's over and I sink deeper under the covers. My mom comes to tell me goodnight and I can tell she doesn't know if she should stay with me or leave me alone. She ends up leaving when I tell her I'm tired, her shoulders relaxing with relief.

"If you need anything—" she says.

"Thanks, Mom. When are we going home?"

She stops in the doorway and looks back at me, worry flashing across her face again. "Let's talk about it tomorrow."

I bite my lip to keep from saying something snarky to her and she walks out, shutting the door gently behind her.

I lie in the dark for a long time, trying to forget the look in Luke's eyes, the way he lashed out and came back in ready to drug me to get what he wanted. I never knew he could be that evil. I hear something and turn, jumping when I see the shadow in my room. I sit up and he steps closer.

"It's me," Raf whispers. "I'm sorry. I didn't mean to

scare you. Trying to be quiet so the parents don't haul my ass out of here."

I exhale a long, shaky breath and he pulls back the covers, getting in beside me. His arms wrap around me, his chest warm against my back, and it's the safest I've felt since escaping Luke.

When Raf speaks, his words have an edge, but I nestle deeper into his arms and let his heat surround me.

"I've been so mad at you. The deepest rage I've ever known, that he could entice you to leave my house and go off to be kidnapped..." His voice is low and sends a chill, but his arms wrap around me tighter.

"You know it isn't that simple."

"When will you learn to ask for help?" he growls into my ear.

"Who would I ask?" I tilt my head back and look at him out of the corner of my eye. "Do you mean *you*?" My tone is mocking, but really, what does he expect? "After the way you've treated me, why would I ever turn to you for help?"

He's quiet and part of me starts to feel bad. The last time I was with Raf, I was the one to leave, he was the one asking me to stay...what does he want from me?

"You're right," he finally says. "I've screwed all of this up so royally, I don't know which way is up half of the time where you're concerned. You have wrecked my life, Gabi. From the day you got here, I've been unable to focus on anyone but you and—" His fingers turn my chin so he can see me better and I shift to face him. His hand moves to my waist and my heart rate picks up.

I couldn't imagine that I'd want anyone so soon after the nightmare of Luke on that bed with those cameras recording our every move, but this is Raf and all rationality goes out the window when it comes to him.

"What are you saying, Raf?"

He leans his forehead on mine and sighs. His peppermint breath heats my cheeks and my eyes close, savoring the moment.

"Rest. We can talk tomorrow. I just want to hold you tonight. Please." He leans back and I stare up at him, touched that he's being so gentle with me.

"We can fight again tomorrow," I whisper.

"I don't want to fight with you ever again, Gabi. That's what I'm trying to say."

He pulls me closer, my head finding the perfect spot on his chest and I wrap my arms around him, my leg going between his. He tickles my back, tracing soft patterns under my shirt, and the last thing I remember before I fall asleep is that everything has been worth it to have this one moment of tenderness with Raf Barron.

When I wake up the next morning, he's gone. But I linger in the covers longer, remembering how spectacular it felt to sleep with him the whole night.

I can't get used to that. It was most definitely a one-off.

In fact, thinking back over everything he said, I'm bracing myself for him to be his normal broody self today. But he said he didn't want to fight with me. Why was he being so sweet?

I get up and take a quick shower. I'm grateful it's a Saturday and I don't have to think about missing one more day of school. I'm going to have so much to catch up on. It's hard not to let the images of that room and Luke's face shake me up. It's playing over and over in my head; each time new sinister things about his face or the way his hands felt against my neck stand out.

I replay Raf's words instead, the feel of his hands on my skin, the way he seemed happy to just hold me. He didn't even kiss me once.

I wish I knew how he felt about me.

Everything about him confuses me.

CHAPTER EIGHTEEN

The doorbell rings before I go down the stairs and I pause and rush back to my room, not wanting to get caught with people first thing. The police should be happy with what I gave them yesterday and whatever else I need to answer can be done through Stefen. He was helpful last night in things running smoothly with the police. I could hear his team talking with them for hours after I came upstairs.

I shiver when I hear my dad's voice. I'd almost put it out of my mind that he was in town and expected to see me today.

My mom's voice rises and I hear Stefen trying to calm her down.

"Jocelyn," my dad calls up the stairs and I freeze. "Come down here."

He's the last person I want to see, but I know I have to. I push my shoulders back and jump when Raf pushes my door open wider.

"Your dad is here to see you," he says.

"I heard." I nod and take a deep breath.

He starts to say something, but my mom steps in the

room and barely glances at Raf. She's anxious and shaky, reaching out for my arm as if to steady herself.

"I tried to hold him off until you got more rest, but if you could come talk to your dad for a little bit. Let him know you're okay."

"Yeah, I will."

I pass Raf and wish I could thank him for staying with me last night, thank him for the best sleep I've had in—I can't remember when. But I go down the stairs instead, and my dad is standing there with one of the police officers that was with him yesterday.

He's holding papers in his hand and Stefen's face is red. My stomach lurches, things suddenly feeling wrong in every way.

"Dad," I say quietly.

He smiles and steps forward, his eyes deceptively kind. I used to relax when I saw him like this, but now it only puts me on guard. I've been fooled by these eyes before.

He hands the papers to me and I look at him instead, waiting to see what he has to say.

"It's all there, sweetheart. The court has awarded me custody. We will leave today. Now, in fact." He smiles and the papers fall out of my hand and onto the floor.

My mom shrieks behind me. "That is not possible. Stefen, *do something.*" She bends down, barely holding up the papers as they shake so hard in her hand. She tries to read it and her eyes spill over with tears.

I feel numb. My body is cold. I close my eyes and feel those dark spots in my vision. Raf's arms surround me and he holds me up.

"Breathe," he whispers.

I do and it helps keep me conscious, but it does nothing to calm me on the inside.

"We will send for anything you might wish to have, but I believe you'll have everything you need at home," my father says.

My mom sobs and reaches out to slap my father, but he catches her wrist in his hand and laughs.

"Sarah. I warned you. You assured me you could take care of our daughter." His lips pinch together as he looks down at her condescendingly. "She got kidnapped on your watch." He points at Stefen and shakes his head. "Some detective you've got here. Couldn't protect either one of you to save his life."

"You put me in the hospital. There is no way a court will let you have her!" she yells.

He lifts his eyebrows and the smile on his face is deadly. "Take another look," he says. "I think you'll find everything in order." He looks at me and opens the door. "Go to the car, Jocelyn."

"I don't go by Jocelyn anymore," I tell him.

"Now that you're not trying to start a new life, you can go back to the name you were given." He crinkles up his nose. "*Gabi* never fit you." His eyes are hard as he looks at Raf's arm around me and Raf's grip tightens. "Hands off, *now*."

Raf looks down at me and I try to convey all the things I haven't been able to say to him before now. It's been a crazy ride between the two of us. To say the least. But the thought of leaving him now—it feels impossible.

"Dad, please don't make me go," I plead. "I can't go back to Vegas. I have friends here, a life. You promised you'd let us have a fresh start. You said you wouldn't hurt Mom again —you haven't kept any of your promises," I choke out. "Please, keep this one. Let me stay here."

He grins at me like I'm amusing him, and I cry harder.

He scoffs and steps forward, motioning for his accomplice, the officer who must be on his payroll, to open the door.

"You want her, you can fight me in court. I'm taking her and there's nothing you can do about it." He pulls me away from Raf and my mom steps forward to hug me. I cry in her hair for a second and then I'm hauled out the door and pushed into a waiting car.

Stefen, Mom, and Raf stand at the door in shock. I sob into my fist and watch them until they're out of sight.

We get on a chartered flight, and I sleepwalk through the motions of buckling my seat belt and telling the flight attendant I don't need anything. She gives me a blanket anyway and I'm grateful, curling up in my seat and leaning my head against the window.

I can't believe this is happening. How did my dad pull this off? And why does he even want me? I thought everything he did was a ploy to get to my mother, and it's possible that's all this is now, except he has to live with me.

I intend to make his life as hellish as possible.

He attempts conversation multiple times throughout the flight and I stare out the window like he's not there. For all of my mom's flaws, she has always been the buffer between my father and me. I hate him for separating us now.

He didn't let me bring anything with me. I don't even have my driver's license. So fucking stupid.

My phone is in my pocket, but I'm smart enough to keep that to myself. Something tells me my dad planned all of that to go down exactly as it did: come to get me first thing in the morning and rush me out of there before I could

stop to think of how to get out of it. He wants me unbal-
anced. It's his favorite sport, to shake up my mom and me.

I close my eyes when he asks me another question and
he slams his hand against the seat in front of him.

I won't make this easy on him.

He wants me to suffer.

I want to make him pay.

CHAPTER NINETEEN

The house is nothing like it was when we left. My father has apparently spent a fortune having it remodeled and it looks even gaudier than it did before. He takes me to my room and if he expects me to exclaim about how great it looks, he's sorely disappointed. I have no reaction whatsoever.

"You'll start school tomorrow. Here, at home. I've hired a private tutor." He points toward the closet. "You have a closet full of new clothes, and you'll have a computer when I know I can trust you." He points to an oversized yellow contraption that I would've liked for a desk when I was six. "Same goes for a phone." He sighs and puts his hands in his pockets when I still don't respond. "We'll make this work, Jocelyn. Luke kidnapped you, for Christ's sake. You really expect me to put up with that shit? You'll live here and graduate, and then we'll talk again. Until then, you're here, and it'd be nice if you showed some gratitude."

I level him with a piercing glare that I feel from the pit of my blackest soul. "You expect me to be grateful when what you're doing is basically the same thing as kidnapping? You're no better than Luke."

"I'm your father," he roars. His fists are clenched at his sides and he steps forward like he'd love nothing more than to knock me flat on my face.

"I don't want to be here," I yell back. "The minute I get a chance, I'm out of here."

"It doesn't have to be like that, but so be it." His face is beet red, but he takes a deep breath and seems to calm down, steepling his fingers in front of his face. "The tutor will be here at 8:30. Be ready or deal with my wrath."

When I don't respond, he stalks out of the room and slams the door. A picture I've never seen of the two of us falls to the floor, the glass from the frame breaking. I leave it there and crawl into the bed. Even this is different than my bed before. What did he do with all my things? Burn them?

I get under the covers and pull it over my head, only then taking my phone out of my pocket. I can't let him know I have this. There are twenty-two missed calls, mostly from my mom, and a few are from Luci and Ashton. I open my texts and there are a ton of them too. The tears start falling.

I answer Luci and Ashton's texts first, telling them both in a group text: **My dad took me back to Vegas. I can't believe this is happening, but trust me, the second I can get out of here, I'll be back.**

Ashton is the first to respond. **What the fuck!**

And then from Luci. **We have to figure something out. I can't have my only friend living across the world.**

I want to be hopeful, but I don't have much left inside.

I let my mom know I made it safely, and make sure to say that Dad doesn't know I have my phone, so to please let me be the one to call. I want to send her snapshots of every-thing he's changed but can't risk it.

Mom: I love you, sweetheart. I'm so sorry I couldn't stop him, but we will do everything we can to get you back as quickly as possible. Don't give up hope.

I save Raf's texts for last, the pain in my chest deep-ening as I think about not seeing him for who knows how long. It almost felt like we were getting somewhere. Who knows, we might've been back at each other's throats by today, but for last night alone, I'm grateful. That one night of feeling cared for by him—it's something that will have to carry me through this.

He doesn't say much, and what he does say is cryptic. I reread it over and over again.

Raf: I wasted so much time. I'm so fucking sorry.

And then: **Be careful. Watch your back every second of every day. Don't trust anyone, Gabi. NO ONE.**

The trembling starts with my hands and I drop the phone and cry into the pillow.

I don't know what to do, but I have to figure out some-thing. I can't stay here.

Minutes or hours pass, it's hard to tell under the covers, but when I pick up the phone again, I text Raf one stupid, inconsequential word.

Okay.

I don't sleep until the early hours of the morning and then it's fitfully. My stomach is growling and as I dose off, I startle in the middle of a nightmare, completely shaken... only to realize it's real and I am back in Vegas with my father.

Around four in the morning, I go through the drawers around the room in search of a phone charger and think I'm striking out until I find an old one of mine in the bathroom cabinet. I plug it in under the bed where it's hidden and charge my phone, setting the alarm next to the bed for eight. And then I really do try my hardest to get some sleep. I need to have my senses about me if I'm going to be dealing with my father. He prides himself on always being a dozen steps ahead of everyone. I need to think like him if I'm going to survive.

When the alarm goes off, I'm finally sleeping and feel like I've been hit over the head. The thought of dealing with *anything* is daunting. My lips tremble as I get out of bed. *Get it together*, I tell myself. I take a quick shower and open my closet to designer clothes. Nothing looks like a home-school outfit, so I put on tight jeans, a lowcut blouse, and a blazer...it's the closest thing to casual I can get. I feel about thirty with this outfit on, but I guess it's cute.

I tuck my phone in my blazer pocket, looking around the room. I should've thought to do it last night, but it'll have to wait now—I need to search the room for hidden cameras.

I put my wet hair in a slicked-back bun on top of my head and shut my bedroom door behind me. I make it downstairs just as the doorbell rings and I open it, as my dad comes up behind me. A blonde bombshell stands out there and she smiles widely at us before coming inside.

"I'm Sage," she says.

She's young, twenty-two or three at the most, and looks like one of my father's porn stars. I'm certain that's exactly what she is.

"This is Jocelyn," my dad says.

"So excited to work with you. Your dad says you're so smart." She's bubbly and I want to groan out loud, but I'm not that rude.

I force a smile and my dad leads us into the living room. Her eyes widen when she sees the ornate wood frame swing in the living room, and I wonder what disgusting things have happened on said swing.

"Wow," she whispers in awe. "Gorgeous." She bumps my arm with her elbow. "You were so lucky to grow up in a home like this."

"That's right. You tell her, Sage. My daughter seems to think it's a tragedy that she's back in Vegas, but this isn't all bad, right?"

Sage laughs, but it falls from her face when she sees that I'm not even smiling.

"Oh." She nods. "You just moved back?"

"You could say that."

She claps her hands together. "Well, I can't wait to hear all about where you've been and to get to know you!"

God, she's so perky. But she genuinely seems nice, so I can't help but return her smile. Maybe she'll help me, or at the least, make this experience a little more tolerable.

I look at my dad. "You can go now. We've got work to do."

Sage laughs like I'm joking and puts her hand over her mouth when my dad glares at me.

"Don't let her out of your sight, Sage," he says. "I can bring breakfast in here since you didn't eat yet, Jocelyn, and lunch will be served at noon. You can work until two and then call it a day."

Sage nods and he leaves the room, the door still wide open. I go behind him and shut the door and a few seconds later, it's opened again.

"The door is to remain open," he says.

I roll my eyes and step back. He has a smug expression when he turns around and walks away.

I grab a bagel and sit across from Sage at the large desk.

"So I'm gathering that you're not happy to be here, and with this being your senior year, I can only imagine that homeschool isn't something you're excited about," she says.

"You gathered correctly."

She smiles sympathetically. "Well, let's see what you know and we can try to make this as easy as possible."

I sigh and nod, taking a small bite of food. "Thank you. That helps."

By the afternoon, we have a good handle on what we need to work on for me to graduate. Sage thinks I'm way ahead and it shouldn't be any problem to finish out the year.

"But I wanted to go to Columbia and I'm missing all the extracurricular things I need to help me get in."

"We'll just have to find those extracurricular things ourselves then. There are plenty of volunteer things we can do. I'll set you up, don't worry."

"What's in this for you? You barely look old enough to be out of college yourself."

"Thanks." She smiles and she really is pretty. "Your father is paying me very well, and I graduated a year ago. I need enough money to continue with my BA, and I'd much rather do this than continue doing porn." She makes a face and her cheeks flush, but her voice is matter of fact.

"Well, I appreciate you doing this. It sounds like you're highly qualified and you seem like a nice person. I need a friend here." I lean closer. "I want to get out of here and if you can help me do that, I will make sure you get more money than you know what to do with."

She laughs and shakes her head like I'm joking. "Your dad said you might say something like that." She pats my hand like a fond older sister. "Don't you worry about me, I'm making great money! And yes, I will get you into Columbia. I've seen your transcripts. You've got what it takes and it'll be so fun. One day at a time."

I study her to see if there's any vindictiveness behind what she's saying or if she really is as clueless as someone as smart her can be...but it seems like my dad has her wrapped around his gold-studded finger.

CHAPTER TWENTY

My dad knows to keep his distance from me for the first few days. I breathe easier when I hear him leave and only go to the living room, the kitchen, and my room while he's out of the house. Right before the time he usually gets home, I take my accumulated snacks and head upstairs, where I remain for the rest of the night. He tries to coax me downstairs for dinner and I refuse.

By day three of avoiding him, he comes to my room and pounds on the door.

Great, he's fed up. Didn't take long.

My dad is known throughout the industry for his temper. He's used it to his advantage. The actors on his sets are professional and get paid well, so they rarely see his worst side, but my mom and I were privy to the underbelly of his darkness. I should know better than to push it, but I'm fed up too. I don't want to be here. He's ruined my life just when it felt like it might be improving, and even worse, *I don't trust him*.

I text my mom every night to let her know I'm okay. And Ashton checks on me every day too, telling me what's happening at school and how much he misses me. I miss him so much.

Raf has been quiet since that first day. I wish I could say it didn't hurt to know he's already set me aside, thrown me out like a dead bouquet...or in his case, a used condom.

I put my head in my hands and groan. The longer I sit in this over-the-top room, the more morbid I become. I listen to my dad pounding and keep ignoring him, thinking about how Sage has quickly grown on me. She's annoyingly perky every day, but it's the only brightness in this morose house.

"I will tear this door down if you don't unlock it," he yells.

I know he means it, so I go to the door and open it, grinning when he trips forward. He looks like he wants to throttle me and it wouldn't be the first time, so I wipe the grin off of my face.

"You will come to dinner every night at six or I will remove the door from the hinges. Keep locking me out and I will simply remove the door." He shrugs like it's no big deal, but he's sweating and breathing hard. Hmm, someone doesn't seem as fit as they were a year ago.

"I will come to dinner, but you can't force me to have a relationship with you," I say. "You can't force me to speak to you. You've taken me against my will and I will *never* want to live here with you."

"We'll see. You'll learn to like it here again," he says smugly. "Come to dinner, *now*. You'll want to hear the news about Luke."

Well, that does get me to the table, just as he knew it would. I'm anxious to hear about anything concerning Luke. I need to know he's not coming after me ever again.

I'm surprised to see two men already seated at the table. They're sipping expensive booze in crystal glasses and stare at me appraisingly as I walk in. I can tell by their smirks that they heard my father yelling at me upstairs and wonder what that says about them.

They both stand and introduce themselves.

"James Mathers," the taller one says.

"Edward Miller," the other says.

I shake their hands and sit down.

"This is Jocelyn." My father glances at me and grins widely. "James and Edward didn't even realize we'd be celebrating tonight when they decided to join us. Luke's bail was denied and his court date has been moved up. He'll be going away for a long time." He opens a bottle of champagne and pours a glass for the four of us. They lift their glasses and wait until I do the same before draining the glasses. I pick up my water instead. My dad knows I went to rehab and must not care if I have a relapse. My face heats with anger. This is the last place I'd ever feel safe enough to try a taste of alcohol again. I know better than to get tipsy with any friends of my father's.

The whole vibe of the night is strange. The three of them talk about trips they've taken and they ask me a lot of questions about Long Island and how I like to spend my time. I can't put my finger on what feels off about them, but as soon as I'm able to do so without setting my father off, I excuse myself from the table.

There's a rush of, "Oh, not so soon. Please don't go."

I direct my words to my dad. "I have homework to do. Thanks for dinner." And I get out of there.

I message Raf when I'm in bed, as always, hidden under the covers when I use my phone. I haven't found any cameras, but I still have the oddest sense that I'm being watched.

Can you look up James Mathers and Edward

Miller? They were at dinner tonight. Weird vibes.

Raf: Don't be alone with them. Ever.

You know them?

Raf: Promise me you won't be anywhere near them.

I can't promise that, but I'll be careful.

Raf: Fuck, Gabi. I hate this.

I feel like Raf has let me see more of who he really is in the few texts we've had and the night he held me than the whole time I've known him. And yet, I'm still in the dark. I still don't *know* anything. I wish he'd talk to me. It would help to hear what he's thinking. Even on the other side of the country, I want to understand why he's pushed me away for so long, why he treated me so horribly, and yet acts like he cares now. Was the whole thing an act? Why wouldn't he tell me now if it was?

And why won't he just say why I need to stay away from James and Edward? Does he know something he's not saying? I don't know why everyone thinks I can't handle the truth, but I'm sick of being the last one to hear anything when I'm the one it affects the most.

It makes me angry at my mom and Raf all over again.

My doorknob rattles a couple of hours later. I sit up in bed and stare at the door, my nerves mangling around in a tailspin. I stay silent, but I pick up the chair by my desk and hold it up, just in case whoever it is gets through the locked door. It rattles for a few minutes and I feel like I'm going to shake out of my skin. I don't think it's my dad because he wouldn't be able to stay so quiet. He'd be yelling by now. James and Edward didn't seem in any hurry to leave. I wonder if they were spending the night. God, what if it's one of them?

I sit down, still holding the chair, when it gets quiet some time later. I rock back and forth but don't feel like I can move from this spot. I lose track of time and when I finally crawl into bed, it's three in the morning. Another sleepless night in my childhood home.

I hate it here.

When my alarm goes off the next morning, I drag myself to the bathroom and let the hot water drench my skin as I stand under the showerhead and try to come up with a plan to escape.

Who cares if my father has custody of me?

It doesn't mean I can't run away.

CHAPTER TWENTY-ONE

Now, all I can think about is running away.

Sage doesn't understand why my dedication to studies has suddenly vanished. I don't tell her it's because I'm no longer her responsibility. Somewhere between the rocking back and forth like a crazy person and my shower this morning, I've decided I can't stay here another night, wondering if someone is going to break into my room and do God knows what. I'm jumpy and tired and can only go through the motions with Sage, in hopes that she will leave early for the day and I can start working on a plan.

I don't know where to go. The first place my father would look for me is Long Island. I don't have a way of getting there, no money, no resources. I had isolated myself with everything that happened with Luke here before, so I don't have any friends that I want to call, no one that I fully trust.

When I think of people I trust, the first people that come to mind are the ones I left behind in Long Island. Ashton, Luci, and yes, even Raf.

Sage taps on the table and I look up at her, caught daydreaming again.

"What's going on with you?" she asks. "You've been staring at that page for twenty minutes. I've said your name at least ten times." She laughs and shakes her head, tapping on her planner. "You've got work to do, missy. We need to visit these places today and you haven't even finished your first assignment yet."

"Where are we going today?" I perk up and look at the list she hands me.

She rolls her eyes, but she's smiling good-naturedly as she hands me a list. I still don't know if one wrong move is going to bring her true colors out or if she's really this nice, but I don't want to find out. I'd like to leave here still thinking Sage is decent.

I study the list of volunteer places—a food shelf, a home for the elderly, a few charity options—and nod before handing it back to her.

"Sorry, I'm distracted. Didn't get much sleep last night. I'll get to work." I lean in a little bit. "You were here before me today. Did you see two men by any chance? Friends of my dad's?"

"Oh, James and Edward were here, yeah. They said they stayed the night because they had too much to drink." Her eyes widen as she pinches her lips together, managing to still look amused. Does anything faze her? "They left with your dad. Why?"

"No reason. I wasn't sure if they stayed the night or not."

I try to focus on my assignments, but my gut is churning, wondering which of them tried to get into my room last night.

Getting out of the house is wonderful. I'm exhausted, but being out in the sunshine and the heat...it feels good. Even seeing how neglected my succulent garden has been since I moved away makes me wonder if I should just try to make the best of the situation here until I can legally leave. But then I remember sitting up in the night, ready to hit someone with a chair and know I need to think of something.

Sage introduces me to her contacts at the different places we go and I'm signed up to help out as soon as next week. Part of me feels guilty that she's going to all of this trouble when I hopefully won't be here, but I have to make everything seem normal, not raise any suspicion.

Sage and I stop at a juice bar before going home and as much as I miss my friends, I have to admit, Sage is good company.

"Oh, you have to try this one," she says. "I'm sure there's nothing healthy about it, but it's gotta be better than ice cream or chocolate, right?"

I order it and she's right, it's delicious.

We drink it outside and the day is gorgeous. I find myself wanting to delay going back to the house for as long as possible, but Sage has already put in overtime.

"You're a great teacher and good company too," I tell her as she drops me off.

"You're so sweet. Thank you. I'll see you in the morning!" She waves and beams.

Not if I can find a way to get the hell out of here.

My dad is in the living room when I walk in, sitting where I usually do my schoolwork. I pause when I see him, wanting to back out of the room, but it's too late. He's spotted me.

"Where were you?" he asks.

"I'm surprised Sage didn't tell you. We went to the places I'll be volunteering."

He nods, and it's only then that I notice the alcohol he's drinking. My stomach sinks. He sets the glass down with a clatter and I take a few steps back. I won't be anywhere near him when he's drinking in the afternoon.

He stands up and moves toward me like he's expecting me to run. "We're waiting for you in the media room," he says.

"Who's *we*?" My voice comes out shaky and I grip my phone inside my pocket, as I keep stepping backward.

"It's not important." He waves a hand and I can't breathe.

The panic is boiling under the surface.

Something isn't right.

"I just need to go to the bathroom first," I tell him. I point upstairs. "I'll be right back."

His head tilts and at first I think he's going to tell me no, I can't, but he takes another swig of his drink and presses his lips together. "Okay, make it fast," he says.

I run upstairs and shut my door, locking it behind me. I race toward the bathroom and pull out my phone, shaking as I sit on top of the toilet seat.

I text Raf.

My dad is acting strange. He's scaring me. It's probably nothing, but I just have a bad feeling.

Raf: Call me.

I can't. He's waiting on me. I'm trying to figure out a way to leave. I just don't know where to go yet.

Raf: I'll work on that. Just get out of there and call me when you're in a safe location. Coffee shop, a mall. Someplace like that. Can you do that?

Okay. Yes.

I hear my dad knocking on my bedroom door and calling me, so I go to the bathroom and flush, washing my hands as I look in the mirror and try to calm down.

You're overreacting. Nothing is going to happen in this house.

I jump when my dad calls my name again.

"Coming."

I tuck my phone under the waistband of my pants and open the door to face my father. He grins and motions for me to follow him. His eyes are drooping, the way he looks when he's had a few drinks. I consider bolting out the front door as we pass it, but in the next thought I berate myself for being so dramatic. I'm sure there's nothing to worry about. It's not even dark yet.

We turn down the hall toward the media room and when he opens the door, he motions for me to go first. I walk into the dimly lit room and he shuts the door behind me. I hear the click of a lock. I turn around to face him and he grins.

"There you are."

I turn to the voice and see James and Edward standing there, shirtless. There's a large bed where our theatre seating used to be and spotlights click on, one by one. It's then that I see the cameras everywhere. James and Edward both walk toward me, James holding out his hand to take mine. I turn to look at my father and he chuckles under his breath.

"Don't look so shocked," he says. "We have some work to catch up on. Luke had a job to do and he was too distracted by you to finish that job. I assure you that these men will make you look your best and we'll be back in business." He steps around me to go to the camera and motions for another man standing in the shadows. "Felix, if you can go ahead and get in place. She'll be dressed within a few minutes and we can get started."

"You-you were working with Luke?" I stare at him, trying to make sense of what is happening right now. "I thought you hated him. I thought that's what caused you to snap—my relationship with Luke, why you finally let me and Mom go—"

"Luke had a simple job and he let his ego get in the way. His stalking tendencies were a surprise, but hey, I tried to make that work for me." He holds a dress up and hands it to me. "Did you know the short time your video with him was up, I made more money on that than your mother's last year in the business?" He grins. "Like mother, like daughter. Only you've got the looks to go even farther than your mother ever did."

"You were working with Luke the whole time?" I'm stuck on that point. I reach out to hold onto the nearest chair, my legs weak.

"He had *one job*, get a new video of you and get out of there. Bastard couldn't even do that. He wanted to prolong everything, wanted to make you suffer." He shakes his head. "He's a fucking idiot. He was supposed to have you for a few hours and he broke the script."

"And what is the script?" I finally say. I feel detached

from my body. I clench the material of the dress between my fingers, *squeeze, squeeze, squeeze*, just to hold onto something real.

"Well, today's script is you put this dress on, and James and Edward will have their fun with you. It's okay if it gets a little rough. Your call really, on how you want to play this."

"You're really okay with watching me have sex? Your own daughter?" Tears run into my lips and I taste the salt. "How are you so evil?"

"When it comes to business, I can detach from it all." He shakes his glass and the glass rattles hauntingly. "How else do you think I was able to watch your mother all those years? Business is business. And it's been hard since your mother left. I'm feeling the loss way more than I should. Time for new blood. That's where you fit in." He laughs and then says loudly, "Everyone in place. Hurry and get dressed, Jocelyn. The clock is ticking."

CHAPTER TWENTY-TWO

I step into a darkened corner, cowering as best I can as I change into this dress. I turn to the wall, reverting to my childish ways and convincing myself that if I can't see them, they can't see me. I leave my phone tucked into my pants as I take them off, and I bend down to pull my shirt off while I check my phone. Raf has called six times.

My hands are shaking as I pull the tight dress over my head, and I stay crouched down while I call Raf back. I don't know if he'll be able to hear anything that's happening, but maybe he'll at least know something's wrong.

"Jocelyn, hurry," my dad says.

I feel hands on my back and freeze, making sure the phone is out of sight before I stand up. It's James and he's leering at me in a way that has my skin crawling.

"Edward and I will make you feel good, don't worry," he says. "It doesn't have to be rough. Your dad was just saying that to make you nervous. We'll follow your lead. It can be as easy or as rough as you make it." He bites his bottom lip and I feel sick.

I follow him to the bed and Edward steps forward then,

his chest against my back, as he pulls my hair to the side and kisses my neck. Every part of my body rejects this.

How did my mom ever do this? Was it really what she wanted? Why didn't I ever ask?

My father tsks in the corner and throws a box of tissues at me. "We won't be able to roll until you dry the tears. Don't act like a baby, Jocelyn. Be the professional you were born to be. Everyone here is counting on you."

I don't know how to get out of this. I push James' hands off of me and then Edward's and try to break free of their large bodies acting as barriers.

"I can't do this," I pant. "I can't." I shake my head and bend down, hyperventilating. I don't know which one of them yanks me up, but it's forceful and the next thing I know, I'm tossed on the bed and my dress is ripped in one fell swoop.

The lights are somehow brighter than they were before, and I know without anything being said that they're already recording. Some sick pervert out there will love the fact that I'm resisting.

James takes off his pants and crawls over me, while Edward comes by my head and pulls his pants down slowly, his dick jutting toward my face. I know what he expects of me and I swear I will bite down on that angry looking thing if I have to.

My panties are pulled down with me kicking and flailing the whole time. It only seems to make both of the men more determined. One holds down my arms while the other works on getting me completely bare. My wrists are secured on either side of the bed with ropes and I use my feet to kick until they're restrained too.

I bare my teeth when Edward tries to kiss me and he backs away, laughing and tweaking my breast instead. It feels like they're winning, and I scream and shake my head as hard as I can, letting the sound pierce the room. The room fills with a different energy and the sounds—loud banging and yelling—are suddenly much louder than I am. At first I think there must be more of them than I realized, but then the bed shifts James gets off of me and a breeze hits my skin as Edward falls to the ground.

Warm hands loosen the rope around my wrists and they fall to my side. Only then do I stop screaming.

"You are under arrest," is being said around the room.

I try to cover myself before I meet the eyes of the person who freed me and lose my breath. "Raf?"

He frees my feet and wraps a blanket around me, hugging me tight. "I'm getting you out of here."

"How did you get here so fast?" I whisper as he picks me up and holds me to his chest.

"We were nearby. Just waiting for the time to come in. Your text today scared me, but when you called, I knew it was time."

I'm too shocked to cry or speak. My mind is spinning a thousand miles an hour. I hold my throat. It hurts.

Raf takes me outside and when we reach the SUV, he sits inside, still holding me. We sit there for a few moments and then he grabs a shirt from the back and hands it to me. I pull it over my head, trying not to flash him. He wraps the blanket tighter around my bare legs. It's humiliating to think about what he saw in that room. The car door is open so we can hear what is being said as my dad and everyone else inside are hauled out in handcuffs.

"I want my lawyer," my dad is shouting.

Stefen is the one who has a grip on my dad and I grasp Raf's hand as I watch my father being stuffed into the back of a cop car. I sag against him and he holds me tight. The weight of everything that's happened to me over the past week and for much longer than that is debilitating.

"I didn't know my dad was capable of such evil," I whisper. "I knew he was capable of a lot but not that."

"I'm so sorry you ever had to know." Something about the ache in his voice breaks me even more.

I try to say something louder, but my voice croaks. Raf puts his hands on my cheeks and turns me to face him.

"My little fighter," he says, leaning his head against mine. "Rest your voice. If we hadn't been here, the whole neighborhood would've come to save you after hearing your scream."

He smiles and I feel like everything is going to be okay.

———

Raf takes me to a hotel and we wait to hear from his dad. My mom is waiting at the hotel and she takes over for Raf with the hugs and relentless attention. It's nice, but I wish I'd had more time with Raf before we were around anyone else. Before we go home and go back to whatever my new life is going to be.

Raf leaves to pick up food. I'm not hungry, but I can't remember the last time I ate.

"I can't believe he'd do that to you," my mom says over and over. "If I'd known, I'd have kidnapped you the first night myself."

"Did he ever force you?" I ask.

"In the beginning, yes. That's...how I got my start in porn." Her face bunches up and she cries hard, loud sobs.

"I thought your career was your choice. I never ever knew. I'm so sorry, Mom. I would've—"

I'm ashamed to say I would've thought of her differently. I would've fought for her harder.

Instead I say, "I would've understood you better."

That makes her cry harder. "It's something I never wanted you to have to understand. I had no idea he was working with Luke."

"What about Stefen? I still don't understand how he fits in all of this."

"He knew your father was abusive with me. He helped me get out of here and to Long Island, and he hired Luke to get the inside information on your father. He needed someone on the inside and Luke wanted to get out of jail faster. Stefen had a lead that your father was connected to a sex trafficking case two years ago. Those two men—James and Edward—were both involved. But he couldn't seem to get any evidence to stick. It was a massive risk and it backfired because Luke was so obsessed with you, it nearly screwed up the whole case."

Raf walks in then and we stop talking. The smell of burgers reminds me I could eat and I take the food he holds out.

He smiles sweetly and looks like a different person than the Raf I've known.

"I'm so glad you're out of there." He sighs and stares at me and I feel my mom studying us both.

I smile and look at her, nervous she'll have a bunch of questions about Raf that I can't answer.

I focus on eating. And after that, I focus on the fact that I'm still not wearing pants. I have the blanket wrapped around me and stand up.

"I'm gonna get a shower. Anything I could wear?" I ask my mom awkwardly. It's weird being with Raf and my mom. I don't feel like I'm doing a very good job of hiding my feelings for him, but I have no idea where we stand. And either way, my mom isn't going to like it.

"I brought a few of your things," she says. "Take your time in the shower. We'll probably have to stay here a few days, or at least until we know what's going to happen with your father."

I cringe. "I really don't want to be here another second. I wanna go home," I whisper.

"I can make sure you get home," Raf says.

My mom turns and looks at him, shaking her head. "Don't make promises you can't keep."

"There's no reason she should have to be here. She's already more than done her part to put her dad away. Everyone needs to back off and let her recover. She's been through enough."

My mom and I both stare at Raf, mouths open.

He swallows hard and stares at me, his eyes a swirling ice blue, but I feel more warmth from him than the hottest desert sun.

I head to the bathroom and turn the shower on, and when I step in, I slide down until I'm sitting directly under the water.

Maybe it can wash my sins away.

CHAPTER TWENTY-THREE

I get to go home sometime in the middle of what my mom and Raf said. We have to stay an uncomfortable night with the three of us in a hotel room while Stefen spends the night at the police station. The next day I answer questions all day long. It's exhausting and degrading and I hate every second, but I want to do all I can to make sure my dad, Luke, James, and Edward are put away for a long, long time.

I hope they rot in prison.

Hateful words for a daughter about her father, but I mean them.

I don't want his perversion to touch one more person.

When we finally pull into Raf's driveway and step inside the drafty house, I don't have the strength to question why we'd be coming here now and not our home. I'll flesh out those answers tomorrow, but for now, that guest bed and I have a date and I can't wait to get started.

After a hot shower, I climb into bed and am almost asleep when Raf sneaks in.

"Wasn't sure you were coming tonight," I whisper when he crawls in, facing me.

His hands find my waist and he tugs me closer to him. "Haven't you noticed that I can't stay away?"

"Thank you for saving me," I whisper.

"I tried to save you so much sooner. The whole drug scene and Luke...well, they complicated everything. I needed you to hate me so you'd leave Longlake and so we'd get all the dirt on your father without you being involved. But then I met you. I kissed you," he leans over and his lips lightly brush mine, "and then I felt what it was like to be inside you for the first time..."

I pull him closer and kiss him hard this time, getting lost in him. When he pulls away, we're both breathing hard.

"I'm crazy about you, Gabi. I'm sorry I've been the worst kind of a bastard to you," he whispers. "I'll probably have to go back to being one tomorrow just to keep our parents off our backs, but—"

I laugh and he covers my mouth with his again. His hands tug my waist tight against him, so I can feel how hard he is. I groan and he gives my tongue a tiny nip.

"Shh," he whispers.

"I don't want you to go back to being a bastard tomorrow. I like this you so much more. Hey...you said you're crazy about me." It's like it's just now penetrated and I feel my heart explode inside my chest. "Is that true? Do you really mean that?" My voice breaks and I'm on the edge of either laughing hysterically or bawling.

"I mean it. I never meant the hate. I needed you as far from me as possible, but that was never going to happen. I couldn't stay away from you, even at the risk of your life, as it turns out. And I don't even want to bring Heidi into this conversation, but it has to be said...she was always a means to an end. When we suspected it was her bringing the drugs in, and she wouldn't touch Toby with a ten-foot pole, I was the stand-in."

"This is all so confusing, but I think I'm starting to get it."

"I worked with my dad...against his will, but I knew too much and he needed my help. He tried to force me more than once to stay out of it, but I couldn't. I was in too deep with you."

"And you're crazy about me," I say against his lips. He smiles and it warms every part of me.

"I am. How do you think you feel about me?" he asks.

"Oh yeah, as much as I've tried to fight it, I feel the same," I whisper. "So much that every awful moment we had felt like death, but every good moment was so good that it sustained me and just made me want you all the more. It overrode everything, the times you were...not as hateful. I felt like the biggest fool though, for giving in to you."

"You were never a fool. I was, every time I lost my mind over you. I should've left you alone and worked harder to resolve all of this. I will never forgive myself for what you went through this past week. Luke, your dad, those men. All of it. I—"

I put my fingers over his lips. "No, don't. We're not going to blame anyone but them. They're the ones who did this, and I want to be free of it. That means letting it go. Starting now."

"You really think you can?"

I lean in to kiss him. "Help me forget," I whisper.

He pulls my shirt off and leans down, his tongue wrapping around my peak. I hiss into his neck before he goes lower and lower, his hands pulling down my shorts.

"Are you sure this is okay?" he asks.

"Yes," I whisper.

For the next hour or so, he makes me forget everything but him and the way he can make me feel. When I explode under his tongue, he just keeps going, until I'm writhing across the bed and begging him to stop. He puts his hand over my mouth and is relentless, making me cry out again and again. I grab a pillow and moan into that when it's too hard to stay quiet. When he finally sinks into me, I'm spent, but he manages to wake me back up until I'm falling over the edge again with him.

I can't believe he admitted how much he cares.

He pulls out a few minutes later and gets rid of the condom. I try to remember that I'll need to do something with that in the morning so my mom doesn't come across that—not that she's ever in my bathroom here, but ew, I don't want her to find it. For now, I'm so exhausted I fall into the deepest sleep. He comes back to bed and situates me in the most perfect spoon position. We sleep so peacefully, I don't have a single nightmare.

He's gone when I wake up, the sun bright in my room. I look at the clock and sit straight up. Eleven o'clock. What in the world?

I take a shower, smiling at the things Raf said last night. The way my body aches in the best way from where he's been.

Which Raf will I see today?

I hope with everything in me that he's the Raf from last night, not the other asshole I know now was all an act.

He sure played that part well.

The doorbell rings before I make it down the stairs and I hear Ashton. I squeal and run down the stairs, practically falling into his arms.

"There's my girl," he yells. "I missed you so much."

"I missed you too." I hug him so hard and then see Raf out of the corner of my eye. His face is hard to read and my stomach drops. Not again.

I pull away from Ashton and smile up at him. His smile is so wide that I laugh out loud.

"Are you really back for good?" he asks.

"Yes, I am. It's been a crazy week, but I am back for good." I hold my hand out to Raf and he looks surprised but takes my hand. "And things are finally right with Raf and me too." I look at Raf and he smiles at me tentatively, almost shy. "Right?"

"Right," Raf says, kissing my knuckles. "Sorry, I was a jealous jerk with you, my brother."

"Damn right you were," Ashton says, laughing. "I was just hoping you'd get your shit together before I stole her from you."

Raf's expression falls and Ashton hits him in the shoulder. "I'm kidding." His smile drops. "But, I will totally knock your ass out if you hurt her again. And I won't hesitate to steal her either, if you don't prove yourself worthy."

"I hear you," Raf says, nodding. "I hear you loud and clear."

They grin at each other and my heart melts.

I hug both of them. "I can't believe this is happening," I say. "Okay, we better stop hugging or I'm gonna start crying again...and I've cried enough for a lifetime."

They both back up and start talking at once. Raf talks

about food and Ashton asks about Luci and we all laugh together. It might take getting used to, the three of us being at ease with each other, but they seem like they're both willing to try. And as for me, it just feels right. The guy I love and my best friend, *our* best friend.

CHAPTER TWENTY-FOUR

I was expecting smiles and the tension to finally be gone when I saw everyone today, not the thick anger I walk into when I enter the kitchen. Raf stands with his arms folded across the chest, with Stefen and my mom sitting across from him at the island.

Guilt flashes across my mom's face when she looks at me, and my heart drops. Something is wrong, I can tell by her eyes. She quickly schools her expression and beams, coming over to wrap her arms around me.

"Hey, sweetie. Did you sleep well?"

My face heats as I think about Raf's body wrapped around mine after the mind-blowing sex. I make the mistake of glancing at him and his smirk sends a pool of want between my legs.

I squeeze my mom back, grateful she can't see my face.

"We need to talk to you guys," Stefen says.

I pull away from my mom and see the look she exchanges with Stefen. I glance at Raf and his jaw is ticking.

"Yeah, you need to not keep her in the dark any longer," he says.

Wow, he is *mad*. What have I missed?

"Are you guys hungry?" Stefen looks at his son. "Too early for pizza?"

"We just had pizza," Raf's tone is short and Stefen frowns at him.

"That's never been a problem before." Stefen laughs.

"Cut the bullshit, Dad. Say what you need to say."

The tension could be cut with a chainsaw.

Stefen holds his hand out, motioning for us to sit at the table. We all move there quietly. I sink into a chair and my mom sits next to me, her hands in her lap.

"I think I'll keep standing," Raf says.

"Suit yourself." Stefen sits down across from me and stares up at Raf. He must not like Raf being so much taller because he stands back up and for the first time since I've met Stefen, he's painfully nervous. "Okay, I know you guys have had a rough start of a friendship, but it seems like you've worked some of that out." He swallows hard and pauses for an awkward moment. "Maybe a little too well, if I'm honest." He sighs. "I'm just gonna come out and say it: your relationship needs to stay one hundred percent platonic. Under no circumstances can the two of you take this little—whatever it is—any further."

Raf's eyes narrow incredulously, and even I am having a hard time comprehending what Stefen is saying. We must not have been doing very well at keeping—whatever we are —a secret.

He starts to speak again and Raf holds up a hand. "No, please don't embarrass yourself any further. You have raised me to be an independent, smart...man...who thinks for himself. I know I'm young, but I'm eighteen and I don't need your permission to be with Gabi."

My mom gasps and turns to me, her face a mix of horror and fury.

"Son, stop right—"

"No, you stop. We care about one another...so much." His cheeks turn pink when he says his next sentence. "I've fallen for her and that's not changing. I followed your rules and treated her like trash and look where that got her. Kidnapped—on your fucking watch! I will never forgive myself for listening to you and not following my gut. I should've never let her out of my sight for a single second, but because of you, I pushed her away every chance I got. She didn't need to leave Longlake to bring down the drug circle—she needed to be in on the truth from the beginning. You both owed her that. *I* owed her that."

I stare at him in awe and when he looks down at me with those eyes that are so much softer than they've been before, I stand up and put my arms around his waist, leaning my head on his chest.

"My God, this is insanity," my mom says. "Jocelyn—"

She shakes her head at me when I try to correct her with Gabi.

"No, I'm not calling you Gabi. You're confused, honey. This has been a traumatic time in a multitude of ways. I won't have you making a rash decision to be with someone. Not right now. And certainly not with him."

Stefen reaches down and puts his hand on my mom's shoulder. She nods and then reaches up to pat his hand. The light hits just right and it's like all of the attention in the room is forced toward the glare of the diamonds she's wearing on her left ring finger.

"Mom, what have you done?"

"Yeah, why don't you tell her what this is really about," Raf says.

I feel like I might throw up. She turns and sees me staring at her ring and swallows hard.

"Stefen and I are married," she says softly. "I did it for you—for us. We needed the protection," she adds. I struggle not to yell at her that we already had that without this farce of a marriage, but she keeps talking, oblivious to how she's offending her new husband in the process. "Which is why you and Raf absolutely cannot be together."

Raf's arms tighten around me and his voice is a low rumble that I feel from his chest. "Like hell we can't."

———

I end up next door in my bedroom. I need time to think, time to process the fact that my mom got married without me. We hashed it out way longer than we needed to, nothing getting resolved in our angry words back and forth.

Raf and I can't help it that our parents are together. *Married.* God. It is gross to think about. But we're not doing anything wrong. No laws are being broken. It will sound taboo when people don't know the situation. My mom will be embarrassed about it, but other than that, who cares?

There's a soft knock on the door and Raf opens the door. "That whole bit about I should've never let you out of my sight...that was as much for my sanity as it was to keep you safe."

"I'm safe now, right? No more surprises lurking? Everyone is going to pay for what they've done and you and I can get on with our lives."

"You mean it? You still want me, even with our little forbidden thing going on here?" His eyes twinkle when he says it and I decide happy Raf is the best thing I've ever seen.

"Oh, I'm definitely into the forbidden thing." I lean up on the bed, getting on my knees as he walks forward and reaches down to bring my lips to his.

He kisses me hard and then gives me a slight push backwards. I fall back on the bed and he groans.

"I can't believe we wasted all this time acting like we hated each other," he says, pulling me lower on the bed and tugging my shirt over my head. He plays with my breast, making my nipples harden under my bra and then lowers to wrap his tongue around the lacy peak.

"Oh, I wasn't completely acting," I say, moaning when his hand squeezes my backside.

"Mmhmm, right. I know. I was the only one acting, and it wasn't like we didn't still have enough sense to get down to business, but...we could've been so much more productive." He pulls my jeans down and grins when he sees my Monday panties. "Wrong day," he says.

"I've been traumatized, remember? I shouldn't have to think about the days of the week too. And for someone so productive, you're being awfully chatty."

"Point taken," he whispers before he gets rid of the future's undies. "Less talking, more action."

His tongue dives into me and I forget about everything but how good he makes me feel.

CHAPTER TWENTY-FIVE

When Monday rolls around, my mom talks to me long enough to tell me that she can take me to school or I can skip. She's furious that Raf and I stayed at our house last night instead of with her and Stefen.

"The teachers all want to do whatever they can to make this easier for you," she says.

"I've missed too much school. I'm ready to finally have a good senior year," I tell her. "Raf will take me."

"Are you at least practicing safe sex, Gabi?" she asks.

I roll my eyes. "Yes. You should know me well enough to not even have to ask that."

"I'm still your mother, you know."

"Yes, you are. We've always been a bit unconventional though, don't you think?" I smirk as I grab a jacket and my backpack.

"Are you going to hold it over my head forever that I got married without letting you know?"

"You left me alone with Raf while there had been threats made toward me. You knew he treated me horribly. Yeah, I might be mad a little longer."

She comes up from behind and looks at me in the mirror. "I love what you're doing with your makeup these days."

I glance at her, surprised that she's complimenting me. She usually has at least one "constructive" criticism to make. "Thanks."

She smiles and jumps when Raf walks into the bathroom with us.

"Time to go," he says.

She crosses her arms and glares at him and I roll my eyes. It's going to take time for all of us. I guess none of us can expect instant peace.

"Bye, Mom."

Her expression softens and she kisses my cheek. "Bye. Come over for dinner tonight?"

I giggle. It is weird that we're in two different houses, but I kind of like it. I'll take it for as long as I can. "Sure, we'll be there."

I grin at Raf and he grins back. He's been a different person since I've been back. Real, honest, raw...and so sweet it makes my heart flutter.

We walk outside and Ashton is leaning against the car.

"Surprise," he says.

Luci lifts her head out of the other side of the car. "Hey! You guys ready?"

"We're going together?" I almost get choked up, my relief to be back thrumming through my veins. Things could've gone down so much worse, but I'm home and...my friends are here.

"We have to stick together at Longlake," Raf says. He puts his hand on Ashton's shoulder and squeezes. "Now, hands off my girl."

Ashton laughs and gives me another huge hug just to piss Raf off. I laugh in his chest and we head to school.

On the way there, I think about how much has passed since that first day that I ran into Raf's car. It's hard to not imagine how things could've been if we'd all handled everything differently, but I've never been about the what-ifs.

I want to live the right now.

It's an alternate reality when I walk down the halls of Longlake with Raf holding my hand, Ashton on the other side of me, and Luci next to him. We walk as a unit, and everyone takes note. With no Heidi around to control the girls and the weight of losing Jen still fresh, the vibe is distinctively welcoming. People that have never looked me in the eye walk by smiling and saying things like "Hey, Gabi" and "Welcome back" and "Love your shoes."

It's surreal.

And *awesome*.

I groan when I see the meal they're serving for lunch. The same lasagna we had on my first day. I smirk when Raf sets his tray down next to me before he sits down. He leans over and kisses me and I know I shouldn't, but I can't resist. I wait until he's sitting and looking at me all swoony, and I reach out and dump his lasagna down his clean white shirt.

"What the fuck?" He looks down at his shirt and then lifts a huge chunk of cheesy, meaty pasta and tosses it in his mouth.

I laugh until I cry. He starts laughing too and the next thing I know, my lasagna is in my lap and he's trying to get bites of *my* pasta. I slap his hand away, laughing until I can't breathe. "Hands off my food."

"Let me eat it, baby," he whispers.

And I lose it more.

Ashton and Luci come over with their trays and look at us like we've lost our minds.

"I'm not sure we should sit here," Ashton says to Luci.

"I'm not missing this," she says, sitting down.

Raf snorts and smears a saucy finger across my lips.

"Gross," I growl. "And I'm actually hungry here."

"Should we let everyone know that you're mine?" he says before he kisses me hard.

I'm pretty sure he gets sauce all in my hair too, but he makes the kiss so good, I don't care.

There's a deep clearing of the throat and I pull away from Raf, mortified when the principal stands there staring at us with two police officers. How did they sneak up on us so fast? I bite my bottom lip and hurriedly wipe my hands and face with the tiny napkin they provide at school.

"Miss Sinclair, if you could follow us to the office, please." Principal Saunders gives me a murderous look and I glare back at him. He's still not on my good side yet.

"Sure. I'd like Raf to join us, please." I stand up and put my hand on Raf's shoulder.

Principal Saunders opens his mouth, about to say no from the look of it, but one of the officers nods.

"That will be fine," he says.

We walk to the office, trailing the three men as Raf squeezes my hand. "It's going to be fine," he whispers. "I'm sure they're just following up on a few questions."

I nod, but my heart is pounding violently and I'm terrified this is bad news. What if Luke or my father have escaped jail? What if Heidi doesn't have to answer for her part in it at all?

When we step inside the office, Toby is sitting there,

along with Stefen. They smile at us, and I instantly feel calmer.

The cop who spoke earlier holds out his hand and introduces himself. "I'm Officer Duplant and this is Officer Stanley. We've worked with Toby and Stefen for almost two years now, trying to get a handle on all the drugs coming into the schools. We just wanted to personally thank you for coming to Principal Saunders about Heidi when you did, Gabi. He came straight to us and it's actually how we connected her to Luke—her preoccupation with you led us to look into her history and when we found out they were related, everything started falling into place. They both have a mile-high stack of charges against them. Heidi will obviously do less time because she's a minor and doesn't have quite the list Luke does, but we will hopefully see justice for Jen's family."

My eyes well with tears and I try to smile instead of sobbing. "I'm really glad I don't have to hate you, Mr. Saunders."

Everyone laughs, Principal Saunders the loudest. "So am I. You drive a hard bargain." He chuckles and shakes his head. "If you can just keep the food fights nonexistent, we'll really be good."

We laugh again and I nod. "I think I can handle that. Thank you for this," I say to the officers and then look at Toby and Stefen. "And thank you for saving me. I don't know if I've thanked you enough for the nightmare you got me out of."

"You have," they both say.

I grin and Mr. Saunders fills out two slips. "In case you need these for your next class. I think the bell's about to ring."

We take them and walk out of the office. I feel a thousand times lighter.

"Skip with me and let's go take a nap? You kept me up all night," Raf whispers into my ear.

I shiver but shake my head. "Not happening. I'm not missing another day of school. Columbia, baby."

He grins and kisses me quickly before we reach the lockers. "Did I tell you I've always wanted to go to Columbia?"

My eyes widen. "You're kidding."

He opens his locker and hanging on the back is a Columbia poster. The edges are crinkled like it's been there a while. So I know he's not just making it up for my sake.

"Meant to be," he says, kissing my cheek.

I smile up at him and know I'm probably looking ridiculously cheesy with how hard I am beaming right now, but I can't contain it.

"I didn't think you could possibly be any more appealing to me than you already are, but I want you so bad right now I could almost skip." My words are reverent, but he presses his lips together to keep from laughing.

"Oh no. We're not skipping a single day. Get to class, Sinclair." He tosses the words over his shoulder and leaves me standing there with my mouth hanging open.

Typical.

EPILOGUE

Fall at Columbia University

I fall on the couch, unloading the contents of my backpack onto the coffee table in front of me.

"I have so much homework."

"Livin' the life," Raf teases. "I think we get as much done as we can tonight so we can play hard once Ashton gets here."

Ashton is already making news with his football career at the University of Alabama. We're supposed to fly there next month to see one of his games, but he's coming in late tonight after a game in Virginia. We haven't seen each other since we started school, but we FaceTime frequently.

I still haven't told Raf Ashton's secret because it's not mine to tell, even though Raf has grilled me on that kiss that happened between Ashton and me many times. It feels like such a long time ago, but it still makes me laugh when I think about it. Ashton was trying to make Raf jealous, but our kiss was so good it surprised both of us. He knows I love

Raf though and knew it then too. What Raf doesn't know is that Ashton also loved *him*.

I think it's safe to say that he's completely moved on now.

"I can't wait for him to get here." I grin at Raf and when his lips part and his eyes darken with lust, I lift up a hand. "Nuh-uh. Wipe that thought from your mind."

"I can be quick," he says, stalking toward me like I'm his prey.

I want to argue about how much work I have to do, but he goes straight for my weak spot. Two orgasms later and I'm feeling much calmer.

"See? Now we can get to work," he says, laughing at my sated grin.

We do manage to get a lot done and when Ashton is due in a few minutes, I'm bouncing near the door, checking the time every few seconds. Our little apartment is just big enough for the two of us, so it's going to be awfully cozy with Ashton and—

The doorbell rings and I clap my hands together. "They're here!" I yelp.

"They're?" Raf asks, holding the door open. He grins and then shoots a look of surprise my way when he sees a tall, *hot* guy standing next to Ashton. Ashton grabs the guy's hand and grins, his eyes a little nervous on Raf.

"This is my boyfriend, Gus," he says shyly.

I hug Gus and then Raf does too, before we even get to Ashton. When I reach Ashton, he whispers, "Well, here goes."

"I've missed you so much." I put my hands on his face and grin until my cheeks hurt.

"I've missed you more."

"You gonna hug me or hog my girl?" Raf asks. They hug each other hard and Raf looks at Gus again, his eyebrows lifting. "So how about we start from the beginning," he says.

We all laugh and head into our tiny living room. I knew Ashton was bringing Gus and have been counting down the days until they got here. The secret has been eating me up inside. I'm thrilled that I don't have to keep it any longer.

"Well, you know since we couldn't *both* have Gabi...and I actually like men too...I thought it was time you knew the truth about me," Ashton says.

I look at Gus, worried he would get the wrong idea about me, but he hangs on Ashton's words and smiles sweetly at me. My shoulders relax and I can't stop smiling the rest of the night. Ashton and Gus are so cute together and it feels like I finally have everything I've ever wanted.

True love with a man I'm crazy about.

I'm at the school of my dreams.

I have a best friend who is happy.

Oh yeah, and my dad will be in prison until he's ancient. Luke too. Turns out the sex trafficking ring was far bigger than we knew and they were neck-deep in it. I was saved from a lifetime of heartache by escaping the two of them.

My mom and Stefen are still annoyed that Raf and I are living together, but we'll go home for the holidays just long enough to appease them.

I'm not living my life by anyone else's rules any longer. And it's working out pretty great so far.

"Life is full of surprises," Raf says. "I'm just happy you're so happy. You deserve a love like Gabi and I have."

He passes around a few beers for them and opens a bottle of sparkling cider for the two of us. I've told him he's free to drink whatever he wants—I honestly don't crave it anymore—but he insists he doesn't miss alcohol and if I can give it up, so can he. It makes me love him all the more. I've never had anyone put me first, ever.

Our glasses and their bottles clank together and I see a vision of our future with many joyful times like this. My adult life is shaping up to be so much better than my child-hood. And all the things I left unsaid for so long, all the time Raf and I wasted trying to stay away from each other, I've learned to leave nothing unspoken.

"You guys changed my life," I say to Raf and Ashton. "I love you so much. And Gus, I've loved you since Ashton told me how the two of you met. Locker room lust, sign me up."

They laugh and I'm complete.

I'm ready to embrace the hell out of this life.

SNEAK PEEK OF BENTLEY

Would you like a sneak peek of *Bentley*, book one of the Love Your Enemy duet? Bentley: https://geni.us/pvq6Awo

Quinn

I pull the blankets over my head when my mother comes in. She's singing. Again. It's not like her voice is bad or anything, it's just obnoxiously cheerful for a Saturday morning.

My *last* Saturday morning to sleep in before school starts next week.

I peek at the clock and put my pillow over my head. She lifts it off and I groan.

"*Mom*. I didn't have to get up for anything today. Why are you waking me up?"

"We were invited to a last-minute brunch this morning and you need to come with us."

"I love you, but please don't make me go."

"You don't even know where it is yet," she says, grinning brightly.

She's always so damn happy, it's exhausting.

"I don't have to know where it is to know I don't want to go."

"Quinn Leilani Livingston, I'm sorry, but you're going. Your dad has been trying to get in with our neighbors for years—"

And that's when I tune her out because I already know who she's going to say and there's no way I can go over there today. I don't even want to go to the banquet tonight, but at least then there will be more people to hide from.

Mom is still rambling away and I try to put the pillow over my head again, but she holds it in her grip.

"— and with the event tonight," she enunciates like she knows I wasn't listening before, "we never expected to be invited to the Hayworths' brunch this morning."

There it is.

"They won't even notice I'm missing," I tell her, but I'm already putting my glasses on and getting up. I can tell by the stubborn glint in her eye that I'm not getting out of it.

"But your father would, and we don't want to disappoint him, do we?"

"No," I mutter as I walk toward the bathroom. And I mean it. My parents don't ask much of me. I'm a good kid and my parents are great—we've all got it pretty easy as far as families go, I'd say.

I just really wanted to sleep in.

I turn the shower on and glance in the mirror, debating what I'll do with my hair. At the last second, I pile it on my head and get in the water.

And with the water pounding onto my skin, I can't deny it any longer. The real reason this brunch sounds like torture is because I'd do just about anything to avoid seeing Bentley Hayworth.

Even his name makes my lip curl in disgust.

The neighbor across the street for the past five years. I first met him in eighth grade and then was horrified to learn that the jerk I'd sat next to in English was my new neighbor.

I've spent every day since making sure I stay out of his way.

Most of the time, I pull it off. I've stayed under the radar at school. I don't have a lot of friends, and the ones I have are nice and smart and quiet...so far from Bentley's crowd, it's not even funny. He, on the other hand, goes out of his way to humiliate me. So I try to be as invisible as possible.

It's not that I'm a wuss or that I'm afraid of him—I'm not. But I like peace, I actually care about school, and it has been the best summer I've had in a long time because I haven't had to see him.

The guy is a self-entitled, rich, condescending prick.

The only thing we have in common is money and even that we handle so differently. It's not something I flaunt for the mere earthlings around me to be envious of, the way he does.

I hear my mom knocking on the bathroom door and I tilt my head back and then jump forward so I don't get my hair wet. *What is her deal?*

I hurry out of the shower and wrap a towel around me as she scurries into the bathroom, holding a sundress that shows more skin than I'm used to.

"You'll look so pretty in this," she says. She waves a yellow dress with wide straps and pink buttons down the center. It's not bad. For a thirty-year-old kindergarten teacher or a five-year-old. "It'll look so pretty with your dark hair." She eyes my hair still on top of my head. "I hope you'll wear it down."

"I'm wearing a dress tonight," I state the obvious.

"So?"

"So, why can't I just be comfortable today?"

"Because we're going to the Hayworths' brunch," she says between gritted teeth. As if I could forget.

"When did you start caring so much about the Hayworths? You never liked Mrs. Hayworth and Mr. Hayworth is a giant—"

I'm about to call him what I called his son when she covers my mouth and we stare at each other in the mirror. She's flushed and I put my glasses back on so I can see her better. We rarely have any kind of altercation. I don't cause trouble, she trusts me, and everyone is happy. It's worked out well for us my whole life.

So I don't know what's happening when she clears her throat and doesn't make eye contact with me as she says her next words.

"Don't argue with me, Quinn. Get over this attitude you have about Mr. Hayworth and his son and look your best, instead of like something the cat dragged in. They've been through a lot. The least you can do is have empathy. A little compassion wouldn't hurt. You can wear your glasses today since you'll be wearing your contacts tonight, but at least do something with your hair besides that rat's nest you've got going on. Make an effort."

Her cheeks have two bright spots on either side. She hangs the dress on the back of my door and leaves the bathroom, leaving me staring after her wondering what she's done with my mother.

I do make an effort since I don't want to embarrass my parents. When I step out and see my mom, my mouth drops. Her long dark hair is down for once and it's in loose waves. I've never seen it quite like this. She always has it up in a chignon and wears neutrals. Today she's wearing a pretty red dress and she looks beautiful.

"Wow, Mom." I whistle and Dad joins in.

She flushes and rolls her eyes but looks pleased. Once she's gotten over that, she looks me over more critically and I wait for her assessment.

She smiles and I relax.

"You look lovely," she says. "The ponytail wouldn't be my first pick, but it's pretty and your makeup looks like you tried."

"High praise. Thanks." I pretend to be more offended than I am. I'm more offended that I have to go to this thing at all.

Dad holds out his hands and Mom and I both take one, heading out the door. There are already cars lining the street, and we maneuver through more coming down the street as we walk to the Hayworth mansion.

I do have compassion where Bentley's mother is concerned. She seemed like an icy personality, nothing ever out of place, and she could look right through you, but every time I saw Bentley with her, she lit up. And he was different around her too. More human.

She died a year ago and the rumor is that she killed herself.

I wouldn't wish that kind of pain on anyone.

Guests are milling about on the lawn and when we walk to the backyard, the view of the ocean is stunning. Tables are set up out there and the water is thrashing about like it doesn't approve of the interruption. I glance around for Bentley, but just then Mr. Hayworth steps in front of us and holds his hand out to take my mother's. He kisses her hand with a flourish, which causes her cheeks to pink up, and then he shakes my dad's hand, pounding him on the back. My dad beams and thanks him for inviting us.

"It's my pleasure. We've needed to get together long before now. I apologize that my work has gotten in the way of that." He glances at me and nods. "Quinn, nice to see you again."

I can't believe he remembers my name. He's barely acknowledged me since the day we met.

I force a smile and groan inside when my dad keeps talking. He sounds so eager.

"Well, you have my vote, Mr. Hayworth. I've been so impressed by what I've seen with your education plan."

"Please, call me Matthew," he says.

And I want to gag. Not because he's saying anything wrong necessarily, but the tone he's using on my dad. This is where Bentley gets his condescension.

I glance around and something catches my attention down the beach, a few yards away. Bentley has a girl leaning against the fence and her leg is hiked up around his waist.

Gross.

But it's hard to look away.

How does he have the nerve to do that at a party with all of these political types hanging around? I look at the crowd and notice a few faces I've seen on banners in people's yards. I'm pretty sure all of our city's wannabe— and some already are—representatives are at this brunch.

What I don't know is why we're here.

I watch Bentley for a few more minutes. It's getting heated over there. And then my mouth hangs open when he pulls back, takes her hand, and with a quick look at his dad, sneaks past. He falters slightly when he sees me watching and holds up his hand, making a shooting motion like he's holding a gun and just shot me.

I roll my eyes and his jaw clenches, eyes doing their best to tear into me. I stand taller and don't blink, which makes him falter slightly and that makes me smile. He runs his hand through his messy hair and stalks to the house, his next prey in his grasp.

Asshole.

The one good thing about this day is that the food looks out of this world. My mom tries to keep me at bay as far as piling on the food on my plate.

"When have you ever seen such a buffet of extravagance?" I ask her under my breath.

"You are causing a scene," she whispers, her hand stopping me from piling on another waffle.

I look around because if there's one thing I know, no one is watching me at this event. But my mother's face is pure tension and distress.

"What is going on with you?" I ask, putting the waffle back. "You're acting so weird."

"Thanks, Quinn. I love you too."

"Oh, come on." I look past her. "Where's Dad?"

She motions to Mr. Hayworth and another man standing with Dad, all in deep conversation. She swallows hard and motions for me to keep moving down the buffet.

"We need to save room for all the food we'll eat tonight. We'll be giving a sizable donation to Mr. Hayworth's campaign tonight and that will draw more attention to us than I'm comfortable with. Try not to add to that today."

I nod, not wanting to make her more uncomfortable than she already is. I add a few slices of bacon and wait for her to finish getting her food before we move to the table together.

I keep watching for Bentley to make another appearance and am relieved when he doesn't. All in all, it's not a bad morning considering I had to get up early for this. The food is divine and any time I get to sit by the ocean is a win.

Now, if I can just get through tonight and seeing Bentley twice in one day.

Click here to keep reading *Bentley*: https://geni.us/ pvq6Awo

ACKNOWLEDGMENTS

A huge thank you to all of you who are reading my books and to anyone who has left a review—thank you so much! Thank you, Christine Estevez, for your sharp eye with editing. Thank you, Jena Brignola, for the amazing covers! And thank you to my family for your love and for your tolerance of my characters taking over sometimes.

ABOUT THE AUTHOR

When Hattie Jude is not reading, she's writing...and when she's not doing either of those things, she wishes she was.

➡️ Follow me on Facebook for book updates.

➡️ Follow me on Instagram.

➡️ Follow me on Tiktok.

➡️ Subscribe to my newsletter for up-to-date info about my books and for ARC opportunities.

facebook.com/HattieJudeAuthor
instagram.com/hattiejudeauthor

ALSO BY HATTIE JUDE

Unwritten: https://geni.us/YHJYB
Unspoken: https://geni.us/2nzN6
The Longlake Duet: https://geni.us/meYv

Bentley: https://geni.us/pvq6Awo
Quinn: https://geni.us/B5Ch
The Love Your Enemy Duet: https://geni.us/PTyo

Traitor: https://geni.us/CjVRf
Thief: https://geni.us/ABzfAe
Lover: https://geni.us/2hSUHR
Loxley Prep series: https://geni.us/SOplJTH
Player, a Loxley Prep novel: https://geni.us/PlayerHattieJude